BE CAREFUL, IT'S MY HEART

KAIT NOLAN

In memory of Daisy. You were a fighter and a joy and I miss you every day.

A LETTER TO READERS

Dear Reader,

This book is set in the Deep South. As such, it contains a great deal of colorful, colloquial, and occasionally grammatically incorrect language. This is a deliberate choice on my part as an author to most accurately represent the region where I have lived my entire life. This book also contains swearing and pre-marital sex between the lead couple, as those things are part of the realistic lives of characters of this generation, and of many of my readers.

If any of these things are not your cup of tea, please consider that you may not be the right audience for this book. There are scores of other books out there that are written with you in mind. In fact, I've got a list of some of my favorite authors who write on the sweeter side on my website at https://kaitnolan.com/on-the-sweeter-side/

If you choose to stick with me, I hope you enjoy!

Happy reading!

Kait

CASTING CALL

"I REALLY APPRECIATE YOUR help with this, Tyler."
Norah Burke passed over the caramel macchiato she'd brought as bribery. "It's so last minute, and I'm going to need all the hands I can get to pull it off."

"It's a whole month away," said Tyler, setting down the coffee and cutting open a box of new cabinet hardware. "We've got time."

"A month in city event planning language is, like, *tomorrow*. But it's so rare Halloween falls on a weekend, and I can't pass up the opportunity to do something."

Sipping the coffee and slipping the knobs and drawer pulls into bins, Tyler listened as her friend laid out the concept she'd developed for a new fall festival.

"It'll be an all-day event. A 5k run/walk in the morning to kick things off—I'll need to come up with some catchy name that will look good on T-shirts, and get sponsors." She made another note. "Then maybe a combination harvest and arts festival on the green. Something that'll bring out the local artisans and farmers. We'll get the businesses around the square to host trick or treating for the kids—which will make the parents happy since it'll be well lit and centralized."

"You should have a station set up for fall pictures," Tyler said. "Something with hay bales and pumpkins so the parents can plunk down their kiddos and get quick pictures. Zach Warren can set up a booth. You could call it Pumpkinpalooza."

"Oh, that's good!" Norah made more notes. "It'll appeal to everybody, even those super religious folks who have some conscientious objection to Halloween."

"I'll be getting in my stock of hay bales and pumpkins next week. I'll talk to Logan to make sure there's plenty fresh for that weekend." Tyler scribbled a reminder for herself as the bell above the door jangled and Lorna Van Buren walked in. "Afternoon, Mrs. Van Buren. Let me know if I can help you with anything."

The older woman waved and headed for the paint section.

"Now here's the part I'm really going to need help with," Norah said. "The old department store is empty. On the market, of course, but it's a huge space and nobody's biting yet. I got the owner to let us use the first floor to make a haunted house. We'll charge a cover to get in, and I'm planning to talk each of the main businesses in town into sponsoring a room, so to speak. Then we'll have the people vote for whichever room is scariest. They'll be responsible for their own costs and materials, but we'll still need to build something to divide up the space."

"The most economical way to do it would be to set up giant fabric partitions. It'd be pretty cheap to do it with PVC. You don't want to create anything permanent, unless you've got some future uses in mind."

"Good point. See, this is why I needed another brain to bounce ideas off of."

Mrs. Van Buren stepped up, several paint brushes in hand. "Oh, I love a good haunted house! Camilla Dixon at The Calico Cottage can order you the fabric. Something black, I'd think. And I bet the Quilting Queens would volunteer to sew them up."

"The Quilting Queens?" Norah asked.

"It's this big inter-church group of ladies who quilt. Nobody has room in their house to host that big a group, so they rotate through the fellowship halls of all the churches in town. They meet once a week and make quilts to donate to folks. You should talk to Nancy McAlpin. She's their current president."

"Come to think of it, they have a lot of PVC frames for their annual show. They might be willing to loan them out," Tyler said.

Norah grinned as she scribbled. "God, I love this town."

Lorna shifted her attention to Tyler. "I wanted to pick your brain. See I have this dresser I want to refinish. Hank already stripped it for me, and I've picked out the color stain I want, but I don't know what kind of brushes I need or what supplies I might be forgetting."

"Let me help you with that." Tyler rose and led her back to the paint supplies.

Ten minutes later she was ringing up Lorna's purchases.

The bell rang again as a brunette whirlwind bounced through the door, singing, "Dust off your dancing shoes, we have a mission."

Tyler barely spared her best friend a glance as she continued to bag up Lorna's varnish, stain, lint-free cloths, and new paint brushes. "Now remember, the natural bristle brushes are for oil-based paint only. These synthetic ones you bought can go for oil or water-based, but for the varnish you're going to use on that dresser, the natural bristles will give you a smoother finish."

The older woman grinned. "This is going to look so good! I'll be sure to take pictures."

"You do that. Be sure to tag us on Facebook!" Tyler called.

"I will!" Lorna waved and pushed her way out the front door of the shop with a jingle.

Piper hopped up on the counter and swung her legs. "Did you hear what I said?" she demanded.

With a bland stare, Tyler passed right by her and continued to stock the new selection of cabinet hardware. "I'm pretty sure you're the only one who remembers I ever *wore* dancing shoes."

"Not the truth and so not the point," Piper insisted.

"And what *is* the point? You know I don't dance anymore." *In public, anyway.*

"You will for this. The Madrigal is in danger."

Tyler paused, a drawer pull in her hand as her heart twisted. The historic Madrigal Theater was an institution in downtown Wishful. It was a central feature of the best memories from her past. Though "past" was the operative term. "That's terrible! But what does it have to do with me?"

"They've agreed to let us make one last effort to raise the money to save it. To prove that it can be a sound investment. Nate is directing a production of *White Christmas*. And you're going to unearth your dancing shoes from whatever graveyard you left them in to audition for it with me."

"You used to dance?" asked Norah with interest.

"I haven't danced or sung since college."

Piper hopped down from the counter and pointed an accusatory finger. "You lie. You've sung and danced with me as recently as last month."

"What we do in the privacy of my living room under the influence of a pitcher of margaritas is between you and me and no one else. And wipe that considering smirk off your face, Norah."

"What smirk?"

"The one that says you're trying to figure out how you can use that in your next community development scheme." She shoved plastic wrapped hardware into the Plexiglas bins with more force than necessary.

"Oh, come on, Tyler," Piper said. "It's not like you've lost your chops. You'd be a shoe-in for Judy. And I would make the perfect Betty."

"Give me one good reason why I should come out of retirement," Tyler said.

"Let's just say, we're doing it for a pal in the Army."

Tyler fisted a hand on her hip and leveled a Look at Piper.

"What? It was appropriate," Piper said, unabashed. "We're doing it in the name of the good old days. Think of how many great memories we have of the Madrigal. Our first show. Our first lead roles. My first kiss, with Robert Hudson in *Meet Me In St. Louis*. Where you first fell in love with—" Piper cut herself off. "Okay, so maybe that one's not good to remind you about, but you can't hold his asshatishness against the Madrigal."

"Whose asshatishness?" Norah inquired.

"He who will not be named," Piper informed her, in a tone that suggested she'd be happy to name and tell Norah all at the first opportunity. As long as it was away from Tyler. Fine. It would save Tyler the trouble.

"I'm not holding anything against the Madrigal," she said. As soon as it was out of her mouth, she knew she'd have to put her dance shoes where her mouth was. She sighed. "When are auditions?"

"Tonight at six."

"Tonight! Piper, I've got to close. I've got nothing to wear here and no time to go home and get my shoes, not to mention I've got nothing prepared for an audition."

"So tell me where your shoes are and what you want, and I'll go by and pick everything up for you."

"I still don't have anything prepared."

"Oh *come on*. As if you can't sing every single number from the show in your sleep."

Given that the two of them had been having sing-a-long viewings of the movie for the last twenty years, this was not deniable.

"It's not the singing part that has me worried."

"Tyler," Piper drew out the plea to five syllables and folded her hands in prayer, complete with the puppy dog eyes that had, over the years, successfully convinced Tyler to go skydiving, be in a bachelorette auction for a hospital fundraiser, and add a set of very purple, very unfortunate highlights to her blonde hair.

Tyler scowled. "You don't fight fair."

"It's the *Madrigal*," Piper insisted.

"Fine. I'll be there, but I'll be a little late. We don't close until six."

"Fabulous! I'll meet you there with your shoes and your outfit. Where are they?"

Tyler sighed. "Top shelf of my closet, in the blue box."

Piper squealed in delight and wrapped Tyler in a rib-cracking hug. "I'll meet you there! Bye, Norah." Without another word, she whirled and bounced out the door.

Tyler stared after her, shaking her head.

"I need to get on too," Norah said. "I've got a meeting with Sandra in half an hour."

"Would that be a meeting with her as mayor or as your future mother-in-law for wedding planning?"

"Some of both. We've taken to planning at the office. When we do it at home, Cam starts looking like he wants to bolt. As if we actually expect him to have some opinion on napkins and invitation designs."

Tyler laughed. "As long as he's learned the valuable lesson of 'Yes dear,' he'll be fine."

Norah grinned. "Exactly."

"If you'll get me a number of how many businesses you expect to volunteer, I'll swing by the site later this week, take some measurements and figure out what you'll need to make the partitions if the Quilting Queens don't have frames you can use."

"I'll let you know as soon as I do. And don't forget, dress shopping this weekend!"

"I'll be there, if only to make sure you don't put me in robin's egg blue."

Norah waved and headed out.

Finished with the display, Tyler hauled the box to the dumpster out back. In the storeroom, she shot a wary look around before executing an experimental series of alsicones. *If only they could see me now,* she thought. *Solid, dependable, Tyler Edison, pillar of the community. Only Piper could get me to do this again in public.*

It wasn't that she had stage fright. There was something glorious about being on stage, under the lights. Putting on someone else's life for a few hours a week during the run of a show. Singing music from bygone days and soaking in the adulation of the crowd. She used to live for it. She used to live for a lot of things. But the days since she felt like arbitrarily bursting into song and dance were long past, put away like childish things. Her life was a good one. And if she felt, from time to time, as if something was missing, it was fleeting.

Still, as the front bell jangled again, Tyler decided it couldn't hurt to take a walk down memory lane in the name of a good cause.

"WE'RE ON A SCHEDULE HERE, guys. Now, I'm not talking about cutting any kind of corners. Quality and safety come first, but I have it on good authority that, if we can pick up the pace and knock this out before Christmas, there's a bonus in it for all of you."

A pleased murmur ran through the crowd.

There, thought Brody, *that got their attention.*

Not that he hadn't *had* their attention. But for the past two days, he'd been ignoring the curious looks, the low-voiced murmurs, the unasked questions lingering in the eyes of the locals who remembered him. He was eager to distract them. Those unasked questions weren't ones he wanted—or even knew *how*—to answer.

"If you've got any questions or concerns," he continued, "or even better, suggestions for how to make this run smoother, I'm in this for the long haul until we're through."

Dismissing the crew back to their labors, Brody decided he

could do with an early lunch. He'd missed breakfast, and the coffee he'd grabbed on the way to the job site had long since worn off. After work today, he really had to make time to go by the grocery and get actual food to stock the kitchen. His forty-eight hours in Wishful had been full of meetings and reports, familiarizing himself with the job, the crew, and all the variables that he needed to tweak to make sure this project was completed on time. It was a strange choice of location for one of Gerald Peyton's projects, but Brody wasn't in the habit of questioning his boss. Project management was what he did best, why Peyton sent him all over the country to pick up the reins on jobs that weren't meeting the company standard. The itinerant lifestyle suited his wanderlust, giving him a new skyline, new faces, new places every few months. It was downright irony that this time the job had brought him home.

And that just made him feel itchy. He'd made a great deal of effort to avoid Wishful, to cut all ties.

He told himself that the fact that he hadn't sold his parents' house wasn't a mark of any lingering attachment. After they'd died, it was easy to let the management company take care of things. The house was paid for, and the monthly income from rent had provided a tidy little boost to his bank account during those lean, first years. He hadn't needed that boost in quite some time, but he was a busy man, and there'd been no opportunity to deal with the house from long distance. He hadn't made an opportunity, he admitted. That the house had been empty for the last six months was convenient, really. He could save up some more money and, at the end of the job, he'd list it with a local Realtor, get the show on the road. The job would only last until the end of the year. Then he'd be off somewhere new for good this time.

He started to head for his truck, to drive out to the highway and the fast food chains that would get him in and out in a hurry, to avoid the million and one things sparking bittersweet memories of his old life here. Disliking the taste of cowardice, he shoved his keys in his pocket and cut across the town green to see what had changed in the last eight years.

The fountain in the center of the green had been dry as a bone when he'd left. Fed somehow or other from Hope Springs on the outskirts of town, the assumption was that the pipes had been damaged. They were near to a hundred and fifty years old, so that wasn't outside the realm of possibility. A trickle of water dribbled out of the stone nymph's flute, dripping steadily down into a shallow pool in the basin. It wasn't a flood, but it was something. Maybe they'd finally sussed out where the blockage was and started the repairs. Brody found himself oddly nostalgic as he took in the coins that winked beneath the water. Wishes. Hundreds of them cast into the water symbolizing hope itself. He'd thrown in his own the day he left town. Maybe the poor saps who'd bought into the legend since then had had better luck.

One hand jingled the change in his pocket. Tugging out a quarter, Brody rolled it along his knuckles, wondering if he should make a new wish.

What would be the point? he thought. *It didn't do me any good the first time.*

He slipped the quarter back into his pocket and strode off the other side of the green.

They'd upgraded Main Street. Brody approved of the stamped concrete now marching the three-block stretch of road in front of a newly refaced City Hall. Charm and function over the formerly crumbling brick that had been in residence when he'd left. Decorative wrought iron street lights provided elegant accents, boasting signs proclaiming Wishful to be *Where Hope Springs Eternal.* Interspersed between them were Bradford pear trees just getting tall enough to dapple the late morning sunlight on the sidewalk. Most of the businesses had been given face lifts. New awnings, shiny new signs, and fresh paint made each shop front stand out like an eager kid on the first day of school. Planters spilled over with bright-faced pansies and petunias. A few seasonally-minded souls had created autumnal displays with hay bales and scarecrows, despite the temperatures that hovered near eighty. September in Mississippi was, after all, still the tail end of summer. Whoever was heading up the community restoration project down here had great taste. The overall effect was charming.

Dinner Belles had a crisp coat of new white paint over the repointed bricks, but as soon as Brody stepped through the glass door to the jingle of a bell, he was back in the past. The black and white checkerboard tiles were worn, but they still shone with a mirrored gleam. The booths were green vinyl now instead of maroon, but they still marched along the outside walls in matching L's that flanked the front door. A smattering of Formica tables dotted the middle. A few of them were occupied—some old timers still camped out with their omnipresent cup of coffee, newspaper, and crossword, and a trio of middle-aged women with shopping bags tucked neatly around their feet. Everybody glanced up as he bypassed the central seating and headed straight for the wide counter in front of the kitchen, but none of them were familiar faces.

Though the lunch hour had barely started, the scents of grease and onions perfumed the air. The smell had Brody salivating as he slid onto a stool and grabbed a menu. The edges were worn and curling, exactly as they should be after generations of patrons' hands. He skimmed the list, idly wondering if the fried pickles would put him in a post lunch coma.

"Well, aren't you a sight for sore eyes."

Brody looked up at the waitress who balanced a tray of dishes on her shoulder. She was looking at him with that expectant air that said she knew him. Scrambling to identify her, he said the only thing he could think of. "Hi."

"Let me just get these on out. I'll be right back to take your order and you can tell me everything you've been up to the last few years." She sashayed away to the shopping ladies.

Her hair was bleached an ashy blonde, with at least an inch of dark roots showing. Her face was angular, only a couple steps up from flat out gaunt, and Brody had the impression she'd been somehow winnowed down. Jeans hugged narrow, almost bony hips. A pack of cigarettes peeked out from her back pocket. Her long nails were painted a bright, bubble gum pink that nearly matched the V-necked shirt she wore.

And he didn't have the first clue who she was.

Maybe she had him confused for somebody else?

Tucking the now empty tray under her arm, she leaned against the counter beside him and laid a hand on his arm. "So tell me, Brody Jensen, where in the world have you been the last eight years?"

The gesture, the invasion of his personal space, solved the mystery.

"Well, Corinne, I've been working, like everybody else, I expect."

She laughed, as if he'd said something brilliantly witty. The scratchy, awkward bray put him in mind of a donkey with strep throat. That hadn't changed much. Neither had her shameless flirtation.

"Silly man, I want *details*." She drew the word out, as if inviting him to share a particularly juicy secret. Her gaze slid, none too subtly, to his left hand. At the lack of a ring, she eased in a little bit closer and his gut wound a little bit tighter with discomfort.

Brody reached to put the menu back, hoping to dislodge her hand. "It's nothing much interesting, I'm afraid." The hand didn't budge. Okay, yeah—lunch was definitely gonna be to go. "Listen, I'd love to stay and chat, but I really just popped in to grab a sandwich to go. Gotta get back to work. Think you could put it on back to the kitchen?"

"For you, cutie pie, anything. What'll it be?" Corinne whipped out a pen and order pad.

He refrained from sighing in relief as he got his arm back.

Rather than the cheeseburger he really wanted, he wracked his brain for something that wouldn't have to be cooked. Sandwich. Cold. "How 'bout a turkey club with chips." His gaze skipped down the counter. A rack with the day's selection of pies took up one corner beside the old-fashioned cash register. Nobody, but nobody, did pie like Mama Pearl. "And a slice of coconut cream pie."

"Comin' right up."

As she circled around to the other side of the counter, Brody eased out a breath. He was nearly thirty. Her behavior should *not* make him just as uncomfortable now as it had in high school. But fact was, Corinne didn't understand about boundaries or didn't respect them, anyway. She'd never been able to accept he just wasn't interested, and in the years through college, that he wasn't available. More often than not, she'd embarrassed them both with her outrageous attempts to get his attention.

As Corinne leaned comfortably on the counter in front of him, angled deliberately to give him a chance to ogle her cleavage, the kitchen door swung open and the Goddess of Pie herself ambled out. "You finish on up here and get on the road," said Mama Pearl. "You gots a long drive to get that youngin' of yours from his daddy."

Well that just wiped the flirtatious smile off Corinne's face. She straightened. "I've got another forty-five minutes left on my shift."

Mama Pearl's placid face didn't shift a bit at her display of conscientiousness. "Won't hurt you none to scoot out a little early. We'll clock you out at your regular time. Nasty storm's comin' in from across the river. You leave a little bit early so you can beat it back. Safer that way."

Corinne started to say something else, but Mama Pearl just rolled right over her. "You go on back, have some lunch before you go. You's too skinny." She pounded a hand on the pass-through. "Omar! You see this girl gets some meat on her."

Outflanked, Corinne stepped back and shot Brody a flirtatious smile. "Looks like I'm out. But you come on back now, you hear? We need to catch up good and proper."

Brody said nothing, just lifted his hand in a half wave as Corinne stepped through the kitchen door. Then he let out a sigh of relief.

Bullet dodged.

Mama Pearl began to wipe the already clean counter in front of him with swift, efficient strokes that telegraphed her irritation. Her fathomless dark eyes pegged him on the stool, made him feel like a kid called to the principal's office. Brody fought the urge to hunch his shoulders.

"Took you long enough," she said at length.

"I'm sorry?"

"You got unfinished business here. 'Bout time you took care of it."

"Order up!" The short order cook slapped a bell and slid the takeout box through the window.

Mama Pearl took her time bagging it, fixing Brody's drink, ringing him up. The better to let him stew in the juices of her disapproval. It might have been stupid to be bothered by that, but he was. As she passed over the bag, Brody wondered how many other folks were going to offer up their opinion about his long absence.

With no particular destination in mind, he started walking again, figuring there'd be a sidewalk bench where he could scarf down his sandwich. He turned off Main Street, noting the swanky new facade and the attractive patio seating they'd added to The Daily Grind, and made his way down Broad Street, toward his old stomping grounds. The restoration project hadn't made it quite this far. The buildings were less well-kept, dingier with age and use. This was the street that came to him in dreams on the rare occasions he thought of home.

Home.

It gave him pause to realize he still thought of Wishful as home, but he'd spent the first two decades and change of his life here, after all. Shoved by a gust of autumn wind, he found himself propelled in front of the Madrigal Theater. It was here Brody was struck by nostalgia for the old and familiar. How many hours, how many nights had he spent here in his youth? He ran his gaze over the building, drinking it in like the sight of a long ago love.

The theater was less majestic than he remembered, huddling now with sedate and faded grandeur. He could see the deep red carpet of the lobby through the front doors, worn in tracks where decades of audiences had trooped through to find their seats. The interior doors into the theater itself were closed and the windows were coated with a film of grime. Stepping back, he surveyed the exterior, noting the ticket window and the poster cases displaying shows of bygone days. *The Music Man. Carousel. South Pacific. Oklahoma!* He'd played Curly in that. And it had been the show that changed everything.

He wondered how many of the old crowd were still here, still acting.

Well, if he were honest with himself, he really only wondered about one member of the old crowd, something he hadn't permitted himself to do in years. It was normal, natural that he'd wonder about her. All his memories of this place were inextricably bound up with Tyler. His perfect leading lady. The one who hadn't wanted to be his lady off stage in the end.

Brody shut down that avenue of thought in a hurry.

What had happened with Tyler was ancient history. He was a grown man. He'd moved on and made a damn good life for himself. And if that life wasn't quite what he'd imagined, well, he was grateful for the continual string of adventures and surprises he'd gotten instead.

Brody shifted his attention up to the marquee, wondering what play was in the works.

Irving Berlin's White Christmas. Auditions Sept. 18, 6 PM.

His mother had loved that movie and all the other musicals of that era. It had been her influence, and that of Danny Kaye, Fred Astaire, and Gene Kelly that had gotten him interested in dancing. Brody hummed a few bars of "The Best Things Happen While You're Dancing" and did a quick step ball change, shuffle, and slide. It felt great. God, if his crew could see him now. Not that he'd ever been one to let a little friendly ribbing keep him from the stage. His itinerant lifestyle had done that for him for years. But he still felt the pull of the lights. The crowds. The music.

Brody did the math. Auditions tonight. Casting next week. The show would open in early December and run for two or three weeks. He'd be in town that long with the hotel job. He'd audition, he decided. See if he still had it in him to slip into somebody else's skin. And maybe, just maybe, it would make him feel comfortable in his own again.

AUDITIONS

TYLER SLIPPED THROUGH THE front doors of the Madrigal and into the relative hush of the lobby. Through the closed doors of the auditorium, she could hear a muted and incredibly off-key version of "Blue Skies". If the guy could dance, she knew Nate would keep him on, put him in the chorus. Men without two left feet were definitely rarer than singers.

She took her time crossing the plush red carpet, waiting for echoes of the heartache that had chased her out of here years before. But she felt only the fluttering excitement in her belly that always preceded an audition. Smiling, she opened the auditorium doors and slipped inside as Mr. "Blue Skies" was exiting stage left.

"Next!" shouted the director. A balding man, somewhere north of fifty, with dark, square-rimmed glasses and the physique of a man ten or fifteen years his junior, Nate Sheffield was set up in the middle section of seats, about five rows back from the stage. He'd been directing musical productions at the Madrigal for well over two decades. He was as much a fixture of the theater as the lights and backdrops.

For a moment Tyler just stood there, closing her eyes and remembering.

It even smelled the same. Like velvet and lemon oil.

Then a familiar voice spoke up from the stage. "I'm Tucker McGee, and I'll be auditioning for the role of Phil."

"What're you singing, Tucker?"

"'Happy Holidays'."

Tyler found herself beaming as someone started the music and Tucker launched into his number, blond hair gleaming beneath the lights like some kind of Hollywood prince. He still had it, she noted—the same happy feet that had helped him charm his way through the ranks of high school girls and made certain he was never without a date to dances. Yeah, she could play opposite him again.

Not wanting to interrupt, she quietly made her way to the front of the theater and headed for the door to back stage. It was like crossing into another world, entering this secret space behind the magic of the show. Climbing the steps with silent feet, she found Piper waiting for her, small duffel bag in hand. "I have us on the list for a double audition. 'Sisters.' We can do that routine in our sleep."

"Do they have fans?" Tyler asked, taking the bag.

"More or less. Stage right. Hurry up and change. We're only a few more slots down the list."

"Good. I need to get through pretty quickly. I've got to pick up Ollie at seven, before Dad's poker game."

Tyler hit the dressing rooms, slipping out of her work clothes and into the leotard and skirt Piper had packed for her. There was no telling where she'd dug that up. It still fit, though. She paused, a hair clip in hand, and studied herself in the bright lights of the mirror. For a moment she saw roses, smelled the scents of makeup and warm curling irons, as a much younger, more idealistic version of herself waited to go on stage for the performance she never dreamed would be her last.

She shrugged off the memory, twisting her hair up off her neck and clipping it into place. No one had made that her last performance but her. And it was time to get over it and get back on that horse. As someone else was finishing up an audition with the "Blessings" number, she slipped on her dance shoes and felt like she'd come home. Singing a series of scales, she began to stretch and limber up.

Piper stuck her head through the dressing room door. "We're on."

Tyler took the offered fan—a blue poster board concoction that had obviously been thrown together in a hurry with duct tape and no small amount imagination—and followed her friend out onto the familiar stage. The floorboards were worn, scuffed by years of feet, marred by residue from tape that indicated places from past performances. Without a backdrop, the stage opened all the way to the black back curtain. The space seemed cavernous. The lights were up, so she couldn't actually see more than the vaguest outline of Nate in his seat.

"Tyler Edison. Well, it's about damn time you came back. Good to see you."

She lifted her hand in a wave.

"I guess I don't have to ask which number you two are doing," he said. "Go on then."

Tyler raised the fan in front of her face and mirrored Piper's position, grinning at her as the music began to play. There was no set, no costumes, no props other than the fans in their hands, but she didn't need any of that to slip into the role of Judy Haynes. She fell into harmony with Piper as if it had been a day, not years, since they'd performed together at something other than karaoke. They played off each other, grinning, glaring, sparking with all the subtle and not so subtle cues that fed the audience and told the story.

God, she'd missed this! Her body felt electrified, alive, fueled by the music.

They finished the routine and danced off stage left to a smattering of applause from those still congregated to see the rest of auditions.

Piper held up a hand for a high five. "Nailed it."

Tyler slapped her hand, followed up with a hip bump. "We've still got it."

~

SHE WAS STILL HERE.

Brody stared at the empty spot on the stage, where Tyler had just flounced off. He'd convinced himself that she'd be long gone, as he had. That there was nothing left for her here. It was how he'd been able to accept the hotel job without so much as blinking.

But there she was, exactly where she should be. It was a sucker punch to the gut. *God.* After all these years, she still left him breathless.

Someone slid into the seat next to him. "Well, if it isn't the ghost of performances past."

Mind reeling, Brody didn't immediately process the voice. He turned his head, stared at the face with the curiously blank expression. Then his brain kicked into gear. The face was older—weren't they all?—and a bit craggier than he remembered.

"Tucker." Brody wanted to smile, but he wasn't sure of his reception. Tyler hadn't been the only one he'd left behind.

"What're you doing here?" There was no accusation in Tucker's tone, just mild interest. It was as good as a shout. The quieter Tucker got, the more pissed he was. And Brody was forced to admit he had a right to be pissed.

"Thought I'd audition," he said, though he knew Tucker hadn't meant here in the theater. "I'm in town for a job for a few months. Thought it'd be good to get back on stage."

Slowly, Tucker nodded. "Your timing's pretty good. We need the big guns to save the Madrigal."

"Save it?"

"It's fallen on pretty hard times, what with the economy being like it is. Old Mr. Stanton died earlier this year and his kids dug into the books. Turns out the place is on the verge of foreclosure. This show is our last ditch effort to try and raise the money to get a reprieve. We could use some of the old magic to pack 'em in."

Spying Tyler leaning over to say something to Nate, Brody sank lower in his chair and called himself a coward. "I'm pretty sure the magic's dead."

"Is that why you left?" For all his moves, Tucker wouldn't dance around the truth.

"No. But it's why she stayed. And why I had to stay away."

Tucker arched an eyebrow. He glanced up front. "Does she know you're back?"

There was no sense in pretending he didn't know who Tucker was talking about. "Does it matter?" said Brody. "Ancient history. We both moved on." Of course she'd moved on. A woman like that wouldn't waste time and wait around. Somebody else would've coaxed her to the altar long before now.

"You with somebody?" Tucker asked pointedly.

"No." As if it mattered.

"Neither is she."

Brody tried to ignore how his heart began to pound at that news. "What are you saying, Tuck?"

"I'm not saying anything. Just stating some facts." Information delivered, Tucker sat back. "Should be a good show. With you here, all the old gang's come out of the woodwork."

"Think it'll be enough?"

"Don't know. But if anybody can pull this off, it's Norah."

"Norah?"

"Cam's fiancée."

"Campbell Crawford is getting married?" Brody tried to wrap his brain around that idea.

At this Tucker grinned. "Yep. Not a local girl, but you'd never know it. Landed here last year, stuck like glue. She's the one behind the rehab downtown. Heading up this whole campaign toward rural tourism. She's really jazzed everybody up for revitalizing the town."

Which meant she was probably somehow behind the hotel. It made a lot more sense now why his boss had chosen this site. He'd gotten on a kick with urban redevelopment the last few years. Perhaps he'd decided on more of a small town angle. It would suit Peyton's give-back attitude.

It was odd to think of Wishful as anything other than dying, as it slowly had been over the last several decades. Brody found he liked the idea of new growth, of projects aimed at restoring his hometown to its former glory days. Even if those glory days had burnt out years before he'd been born.

"Hey Twinkle Toes McGee, get up here for a reading!" Nate shouted.

"I'm up." Tucker started to rise.

"Tucker." Now Brody's lips did curve into a smile as he uncurled the hand clenching the armrest, offered it. "It's really good to see you, man."

After a moment's hesitation, his old friend took it, pulling him in for a back-thumping hug. "Welcome home, boy-o."

And just like that, things slid into place, his old best friend accepting his presence without further question. With him, at least, Brody's return wouldn't be complicated. That would ease his transition back into the community somewhat. As Tucker climbed out of his seat and headed for the stage where Tyler waited, a script in hand, Brody wished his other relationships could be repaired so easily. Then he cursed himself as an idiot.

She'd made her answer crystal clear eight years ago. At best, he was chasing after a memory of what used to be. Which made him nothing more than the romantic fool who'd thought she'd follow him to the ends of the earth. He'd learned better. He couldn't allow himself to be ruled by nostalgia for the next few months. No, he'd audition, help save the theater as his good deed. And finally get some closure so when he left at the end of the year, he could finally move on with his life.

9 WEEKS 'TIL SHOW

TYLER FELT A TWINGE of instinctive annoyance at the sight of Corinne Dawson stepping into the shop, then immediately chastised herself. This wasn't high school, or even college. They were grown women. The crap from years past didn't matter anymore. So she had a friendly smile pasted on as Corinne crossed to the counter, her little boy in tow.

"Hey there, Corinne." Tyler shifted the smile to her son. "Hi, Kurt."

Kurt pressed his face against his mother's leg, but Tyler could just see the edges of a shy smile.

Corinne glanced around the empty store. "Slow day?"

Tyler tried to tell herself that wasn't some kind of criticism or gloat. "We get a lull this time of day. Was there something I could help you with?"

"Well, I hope so. See, I've been on Pinterest."

Tyler laughed. "Famous last words. I think I have about a thousand projects pinned that I'll never get to." *See, easy. Friendly. Common ground. This isn't so bad.* "What in particular caught your eye?"

Kurt began to tug at Corinne's pants leg as she dug around in her purse. "Not right now, baby."

"I bet you like trucks," Tyler said.

Kurt looked up at her. Big brown eyes dominated his thin face. He nodded solemnly.

"I've got a few trucks over here if you'd like to play with them. If it's okay with your mom." She glanced at Corinne, who looked startled for a moment before giving a go ahead wave.

Tyler retrieved the old wooden toys from the office and set Kurt up on the rug by the consult area. Despite his earlier bashfulness, he dove into the trucks with gusto, making engine and crashing noises. She grinned, "He's totally adorable, Corinne."

"All his daddy's charm, none of his bad temper," Corinne agreed.

Not for the first time, Tyler wondered if Corinne's ex-husband had abused her. She felt a stirring of sympathy. No matter how hateful Corinne had been when she was younger, nobody deserved that.

"So there's this little hanging herb garden thing they made outta Mason jars," Corinne began. "I've got the board to mount them on, but I need these clamp things."

"Oh I've seen that one. Cool project. Great when you have limited space by a window." Tyler asked a few more questions and helped her pick out the necessary clamps, along with a small tin of chalkboard paint to make space for labels on each jar. Conscious that errands with a small child could often turn hellish in a second, Tyler was quick about ringing her up. "It's a little late in the year to start herbs from seeds, but I know for a fact Cecil Pryor has an enormous herb garden and loves sharing."

"I'll remember that." Corinne glanced at the door for the fifth or sixth time since she came in. "Listen, Tyler, there's something I think you ought to know."

"Oh?"

"I mean, maybe you already know, but in case you didn't, I didn't think it right you be taken unawares."

Where's she going with this? Tyler waited, eyebrows raised.

"Brody came in to the cafe yesterday."

The words struck Tyler like a blow.

"You didn't know." Corinne twisted the strap of her purse. "I thought maybe he'd come back to see you."

She actually looked…distressed? Or maybe that was just Tyler filtering through her own upset.

"Nate's posted the cast list!" sang Piper as she bounced through the door with a jingle. "Tucker just called. How close are you to lunch?"

"I—"

"Tyler? Honey, what's wrong?" Piper skirted around the counter.

At the touch of her hand, Tyler felt her knees wobble. Determined, she locked them and firmed her mouth. "It's nothing important."

Piper turned, saw Corinne. Defensive temper leapt in her eyes. "What did you do?"

Tyler curled her hand around Piper's arm and squeezed in warning before she could pop off. "Thanks for coming in, Corinne. I hope your herb garden project turns out well."

With another look of what might have been sympathy, Corinne called to her son. "Come on, Kurt. Time to go."

Seeing the child, Piper held her tongue until the pair of them left. As soon as the door shut, she said, "What did that vindictive bitch say to you?"

"Wasn't her," Tyler managed. Too overwhelmed to get into Corinne's apparent change of heart, she simply folded, sinking to the floor behind the counter. It was good that the store was empty just now, good that no one but Piper was here to see her carefully constructed control crumble to dust. The ache bloomed in her chest, pressing, twisting until she could hardly breathe.

Piper knelt down, took her hands and waited.

I will not cry. I will not. Damn it, I won't shed another tear over him. Tyler dug deep, reaching for the stubborn pride that had gotten her through the first brutal years.

"Brody's back." If her voice shook on that pronouncement, at least she wasn't sobbing.

Piper plopped down on the floor and pulled her into a tight hug. "Have you seen him?"

"No." Because he hadn't come back for her.

"Then maybe she's lying."

"Why would she? Why now, unless he really is here? He's the reason she's always hated me."

"Then you'll deal. You've been dealing just fine the last eight years."

"Well, the last six anyway. I don't think either of us is under any illusions that I was fine at the beginning."

As the back door opened, Tyler brushed at her face, though there were no tears to erase. "That'll be Morgan. Let me just take a minute, then we'll go meet Tucker."

It helped to slide back into normal, to give Morgan details about what orders had come in, who needed to be notified. As Tyler slipped into the back to retrieve her purse, she imagined building a wall around herself again. Nothing about this could touch her. Which was an absolute lie. But once upon a time, she'd been a damned fine actress. She could play this role.

"It's going to be so nice to have you back on stage," said Piper, linking her arm through Tyler's.

"You're making the assumption I actually got cast."

"Oh, don't be silly. Of course you got cast. What's with the doom and gloom? Are you regretting auditioning?"

"No. Not really. It's just a little bit bittersweet."

Piper was wise enough not to mention Brody.

"I spent all those years not performing, and this might be the last show."

"Have faith, dear one! The Madrigal will prevail! We will pull this off. You'll see."

That was Piper. The eternal optimist.

They rounded the corner onto Broad Street and saw Tucker waiting for them up the next block in front of the theater. He was bouncing impatiently on his feet, back to the doors. As soon as he caught sight of them, he made big waving circles of his arms, urging them to hurry up. Though she really wanted to go slow, to prepare herself, Tyler gave in to Piper's urging and sped up her pace. Then they were there, in front of the doors. In her periphery, Tyler could see the printed page taped to the inside of the glass.

"Have you looked?" Piper demanded.

"I was a good boy," Tucker informed her.

"Okay then," she said, taking his hand and Tyler's. "Together. On three. One. Two. Three."

As one, they turned and marched to the door, crowding shoulder to shoulder to read the tiny print.

Bob Wallace would be played by Myles Stuart. Nobody Tyler knew.

There, second from the top, *Phil Davis-Tucker McGee.*

Next line down, *Betty Haynes-Piper Parish.*

And after that...

Judy Haynes-Tyler Edison.

Tucker and Piper whooped. Tyler felt something in her unclench. She'd gotten the part. All those years off hadn't actually ruined her abilities. Relieved, excited, she scanned the rest of the cast list, noting familiar names from shows gone by, and a few new ones, too. And then she ran across a name that shouldn't have been there at all.

"Is this some kind of joke?" Her voice sounded hard and brittle to her own ears.

Piper and Tucker stopped dancing around behind her and came to peer back at the list. "What?" asked Piper.

"Phil's understudy," Tyler bit out.

As soon as Piper hissed a breath, Tyler knew she hadn't misread it.

Phil Davis Understudy-Brody Jensen.

"This isn't funny," she said. "What the hell is Nate pulling?"

"It's not meant to be funny," said Tucker. "He showed up for auditions."

"How? I was there, Tucker. I didn't see him."

"You left early," he said, shrugging.

Goddamn it, he's going to ruin this for me too. It took everything in her not to rock back and lean against the doors for support.

"And you didn't think it wise to maybe mention it?" Tyler glared at him.

"I didn't want to upset you," said Tucker gently. And she hated it. Hated that he saw the need to be gentle about this. Hated that there *was* a need to be gentle.

Piper put an arm around her. "Too late for that. Corinne came in the shop to drop the bomb that he was back. It would've been better coming from you."

"Shit."

Tyler closed her eyes and waited for the world to settle again. This wasn't okay. This was so far beyond not okay. How *dare* he show up now, after all these years. How dare he audition for the show as if nothing had happened, as if he hadn't disappeared without a word, without a trace, without a freaking *goodbye.*

She steeled her spine. It didn't matter. *He* didn't matter.

"It's fine," she said. "It's fine." If she said it enough, it would become true. "The theater is what matters here. The show. I'm not going to let a little bit of history ruin the Madrigal's chances." Now that she knew he was back, she wouldn't be surprised when she saw him again. She could play it cool, show that she'd moved on. Because, damn it, she *had* moved on. And she was going to use the next three months to prove it, starting with maintaining their post-casting ritual.

Tyler squared her shoulders. "Let's go get those milkshakes."

~

BRODY WAS NOT uncomfortable on stage. He'd made his debut as Oliver when he was eight and never looked back. He enjoyed the lights, the music, the applause. And never once had he balked because of stage fright.

But on the first night of rehearsals for *White Christmas*, his stomach flopped around like a beached tuna. *Stupid,* he told himself. *Foolish.* Yet none of the tension eased as he slipped in through the familiar lobby doors and made his way into the auditorium. The rest of the cast was congregating at the front, beside the orchestra pit. They were laughing, joking. A few folks were singing. And there was Tyler up on stage, already running through some choreography with Tucker.

Unlike the night of auditions, the auditorium was well lit, so when she came out of her spin facing the back, she saw him and went utterly motionless, the smile on her face fading. Tucker followed her gaze. Dimly, Brody was aware of him nodding a greeting, but he didn't return it. He was too busy trying to get his breath back. He felt the punch of her gaze all the way at the back of the room, his feet seeming to root to the spot as he stared back at her. She wasn't surprised to see him. She'd have read the cast list and known he was coming. Her usually expressive face was carefully blank, giving him no clues as to what she was thinking or feeling. And that was as alien and unfamiliar as his own nerves.

A loud pop of floorboards interrupted the silence as a couple dozen eyes kept shifting from her to him, waiting for someone to break the stalemate.

Nate did the honors, giving a ching-a-ring on the piano to get everyone's attention. "Gather around everybody. We have a project list and a schedule to go over before we get started."

Tyler's attention shifted to the director, and suddenly Brody could move again. So he did, making his way down the aisle and into the congregated actors and musicians. He shook some hands, whispered quiet thank yous to the various people who welcomed him back. But even as Nate spoke, discussing who was on set building, when the work days would be, when the external rehearsals for the orchestra were scheduled, and other miscellany associated with the start of a show, Brody found his attention pulled unerringly to Tyler.

She didn't look at him. By all evidence, she was focused on Nate, on the show. But he had a feeling that she was aware of him, that she knew his position in the crowd if for no other reason than to avoid looking at him. He took the opportunity to look his fill at her, cataloging the changes, the differences.

Her honey blonde hair was scraped back into a prim ballerina's bun, but slippery strands were already escaping to frame her face, to soften the long line of her neck. That hair would feel like silk. The memory of it sliding through his fingers made his hands clench. Her face was a little bit sharper now, more serious, but no less appealing. Where her face had sharpened, her body had softened. Not in an unhealthy way. She was still every bit as trim and fit as she'd been in college. But her hips were a little fuller, her curves more gently rounded, and well displayed by the form-fitting yoga pants and t-shirt she wore. Which wouldn't have been her intention. She'd want comfort and ease of motion.

"...choreographer will be here on Friday, so the name of the game this week is to learn all your music and start learning your lines. The schedule is in your script packets." Nate picked one up, waved it. "Now, if any of you are familiar with the actual stage production of *White Christmas The Musical*, you will know that it bears little resemblance to the movie we all know and love. I chose this show based on nostalgia. *White Christmas* is my favorite Christmas movie, and it's incredibly well-known. People hear we're putting on a production, *that's* the story they expect to see. So I contacted the Irving Berlin estate and requested permission to make my own adaptation of the movie script. Given we are a town of less than five thousand, they don't have a lot of fear this will become a raging success, so they actually said yes. That said, it's a one shot deal. We get one three week run of the show, and that's that. Permanently retired after that. But at least we'll be adhering as faithfully as possible to the actual plot and script of the movie, with minor changes to facilitate our set limitations. So come and get 'em and let's get started."

Well that'll make lines that much easier to learn, thought Brody. *White Christmas* had been an annual tradition with his mother.

Brody got in line with the others, taking advantage of the general milling and conversation to wend his way forward, closer to Tyler. He wasn't sure exactly what he was doing. Testing himself, or maybe her.

"Hey, Tyler."

She stood very straight, very still, not budging when the line in front of her moved.

Brody circled around her, offered a smile.

Those clear gray eyes were icy, distant. "Brody." Her tone was flat—not accusatory, but not welcoming, either. In a woman he'd once believed embodied warmth and generosity, it felt like a slap. He wasn't sure what he should've expected, but it wasn't this.

"You look good," he said.

She made a noncommittal noise and edged forward, hand outstretched to take her script packet from Barbara Monahan, the pianist. Barbara offered him a raised eyebrow and mouthed *Good luck* as he took his packet. He flashed her an appreciative look and followed Tyler.

"It's good to see you," he said, and it was, despite the awkwardness and the questions that hung between them. He'd missed her. He hadn't truly realized how much until seeing her again.

But she didn't say the same, and that was a puzzle. It'd been her decision to stay, after all.

There was a wound between them. Brody could feel it pulsing

like a bruise. He wondered if they had it out now, as they hadn't eight years ago, would the wound bleed free and clean, purging them both of whatever pain they'd been carrying around? It hadn't been a messy breakup. Not because they hadn't loved. It had simply been that they wanted different things. Her silence had made that clear enough. And maybe that was worse than a messy breakup.

Tucker and Piper, heads together, shot him a sympathetic look. Brody wasn't sure if that meant they were on his side or were pitying his stupidity. Not that he was even sure what his side was. He wanted closure, he supposed. The resolution he hadn't gotten all those years before. And that meant Tyler was going to have to talk to him. Sooner or later.

"I REALLY APPRECIATE YOU helping us out with materials." Nate slid the top sheet of plywood from the stack.

Tyler hefted the other end and helped him carry it into the workshop behind the theater. "Being the boss has a few benefits. Among them, the ability to apply my employee discount perhaps a bit more liberally than is appropriate." Business at the hardware store had been good this year with all the face lifts and upgrades folks were giving to their storefronts and homes. She could afford to take the hit of giving the show building materials almost at cost. It was for a good cause, after all.

Her eyes automatically flicked toward Brody as his laugh rolled out, rich and rollicking. He and Tucker danced around, mock boxing, egging each other on with insults delivered in every accent from Cockney to Russian as they headed back out for the next sheet. Irritation prickled. He'd slipped back in so damned easily with everyone—horsing around, joking, diving in as if it had been eight days instead of eight years since he'd seen them last. As if he hadn't abandoned *them* too.

He'd continued to make friendly overtures to her, which good manners dictated she didn't continually rebuff.

Yeah, right.

It was good manners, taking the high road, and not that some part of her was so pitifully happy to see him again, she didn't care what the circumstances were. If she kept telling herself that, it would be true. So far her fake it 'til you make it strategy had been an epic failure. Because Brody hadn't changed, not in any of the ways she'd expected. He was, for all intents and purposes, exactly as he'd been when she'd fallen in love with him years ago. And that made him damned hard to resist.

Not that he was making *romantic* overtures. And not that it mattered if he had because he'd be leaving again as soon as the show and his job were finished. She'd heard that much through the grapevine.

It would only be two and a half months. She could be the bigger person and tolerate the confusion and longing of this semi-uncomfortable distance for that long. As the understudy, she wouldn't be kissing *him*. Thank God.

"Tucker!" Piper's scream echoed from the loading dock.

Tyler raced outside, Nate hot on her heels.

On the ground beside her truck, Tucker was curled in a ball, arms wrapped protectively around his leg, swearing a blue streak.

Piper was crouched beside him. "Let me see." Her voice was no-nonsense, the trained nurse replacing her usual playful attitude.

"It hurts. Christ, it hurts."

"What happened?" Nate demanded.

"We were just fooling around," Tucker groaned. "Doing spin kicks off the back of the truck."

"You *are* aware you aren't twenty-one anymore?" Tyler ran a hand down his rigid back.

"Brody can still do it," he muttered.

Tyler fixed him with an accusatory stare. *This is all your fault,* she thought.

He held his hands up in a *What could I do?* gesture.

"It's broken," Piper announced. "I can feel the bump in the bone."

"It can't be broken. I have to dance." Tucker tried to stand, using Brody and Piper to lever himself up. But as soon as he tried putting weight on it, the leg buckled and he howled.

"Get him in my back seat," Piper said. "I'll take him to the emergency room."

"I don't wanna go to the ER."

"Then you shouldn't have broken your leg on a Saturday," she said practically.

Tucker looked miserably at Nate. "Sorry. I would never have tried it if I didn't think I could pull it off."

Nate scrubbed both hands over his red and gray beard as if he could wipe away the disappointment. "It's all right. You just get yourself taken care of. This is why we have understudies."

Understudies.

Tyler's blood went cold as she reluctantly lifted her eyes to Brody. Her new leading man.

Crap.

They locked gazes for one long, humming beat. Then he was turning away, helping lever Tucker into Piper's car. Tyler reached up and rubbed at the sudden ache in her chest.

Things were about to get up close and personal in a big way. It was one thing to keep Brody on the periphery as just another cast member. It was quite another to be playing opposite him, running lines, working on choreography. Kissing.

"Let's get this truck unloaded," Nate called.

The rest of the cast members, who'd been hanging around the loading dock watching the drama unfold, sprang into motion again.

Tyler still didn't move. *I can't do this*, she thought. *I can't go back here. Not even for the Madrigal.*

Then Nate turned to her. "Thank God it happened early so we're not having to pull a substitution right before opening night."

Now's the time to back out. Just bow out gracefully and let Charlotte step in. The understudies can take over.

Except then everyone would know she was a coward. Afraid to get back on stage with the man she'd once made magic with. Letting her personal issues get in the way of the mission at hand. Failing everyone.

Tyler stiffened her spine. She could do this. She *would* do this.

In the wake of Piper's brake lights, Brody crossed to the loading dock. If he'd seemed smug or pleased somehow to be put in this position, Tyler would've felt compelled to kick him or, at the very least, give him a sound lashing with her tongue. But he looked contrite, worried over his friend.

"I've never seen him miss the landing before."

"A lot's changed in the last eight years," she said. "Tucker's not quite as spry as he used to be."

They both knew that wasn't what she was thinking.

"Truck's empty," Nate said. "Let's get to rehearsal."

Brody gestured toward the stairs, a sweeping, courteous motion. "After you, Miss Haynes."

Tyler swept past him, doing her best to categorize him only as Phil Davis, comedic half of Wallace and Davis. But no matter how many roles she'd seen him play, Tyler only ever saw Brody.

"Okay, let's see where you are, Brody," Nate called. "'The Best Things Happen While You're Dancing', from the top."

Tyler lifted a finger for them to wait and put her head together with Mitch Campbell over some plans for their inn backdrop. Brody knew the architect from way back. He was Cam's cousin, and a few years older than Brody, Tucker, and Cam. Mitch had volunteered to head up set construction for the show, which meant wrangling all the untrained help.

More power to him. He didn't envy the man that job. He did envy the easy smile Tyler shot Mitch before clapping him on the back and moving to take up her position on stage. She'd smiled at him like that once upon a time.

She didn't smile now as he crossed the stage. Her face was set in a carefully neutral expression. Fine. He could be every bit as professional as she could. Brody reached for her, curving one hand around her waist, the other taking her free hand. They fit. They'd always fit.

Somebody queued up the music. Tyler glanced down as if checking the position of their feet, which was ridiculous, since she knew exactly where her feet were in the pitch black dark. The faint trace of color high in her cheeks gave her away. So she wasn't as unaffected as she wanted him to believe. Brody could see the thrum of her pulse at the base of her throat, felt the answering echo of his own as she lifted her head again, focusing on his eyes.

She was stiff at first, resisting his lead. They stumbled a few times. He missed several steps. Then she did. And then the song was over, and she was frowning, knowing they botched the number.

"Okay, try it again, and this time, Tyler, remember you aren't doing an impression of a fence post. Loosen up," Nate ordered.

She took a moment, closed her eyes as if to center herself, then nodded. With a roll of her neck, she shook out all her limbs. Brody felt the difference in her posture as soon as she took position again. The music swelled, and they locked eyes. On cue, they began to move, and at last, at long last, he felt like he was home. Everyone and everything faded except the music and the woman in his arms.

He led, spun, dipped, and by the time she broke away into a

quick shuffle tap, her eyes were sparking with fun and her cheeks were flushed with exertion. Brody found himself grinning, improvising in response, as he couldn't remember this section of choreography to save his soul. He watched her, starting to follow her lead, mimicking, mirroring as they came back together and whirled around the stage. And at last they ended, Tyler in a deep dip over his knee, her face flushed and smiling, her chest heaving.

"Excellent!" Nate clapped. "You're remembering how to move together."

Something hot and dark flashed in Tyler's eyes. Brody tugged her up, into his arms, and held her a moment too long, letting the awareness, the heat sink in. No, he hadn't forgotten what it was to move with her—on stage or in the dark. Neither had she.

Her breathing faltered and she tugged away like he'd shocked her. She looked flustered and wary, which she'd never been at any point in their courtship. It was kind of adorable. Brody was wise enough to repress a smile.

Eight years had done nothing to dim the chemistry between them. She clearly hadn't expected that and didn't know what to do with it, so the default response was retreat. But before her brain had kicked back in, she'd been smiling, having fun, just like they used to. He could work with that.

He took a moment, absorbing the fact that he *wanted* to work with that. He wanted to pursue this, pursue her. Again. He'd think about the wisdom of that later, when he wasn't in close enough proximity that the scent of her fogged his brain.

As one half of the Haynes sisters was missing, Nate made adjustments to the rehearsal schedule, putting the focus on Brody and Tyler, while other cast members and volunteers provided an ongoing backdrop of power tools and paint fumes. Tyler kept fumbling over her lines, having to pull out the script.

"You and your stupid eidetic memory," she muttered, glaring at him.

"I can help you run lines outside rehearsals," Brody offered. "You always did better away from all the distractions."

"No." The word snapped out, sharper than she'd intended, judging by the flags of color that rose on her cheeks.

"Afraid to be alone with me, Tyler?" he teased.

"Of course not," she said. But she wouldn't meet his eyes.

The chorus of "Defying Gravity" from *Wicked* rang out.

"Your ass is ringing," he said.

That earned him another glare as she whipped the phone out of her back pocket and glanced at the screen. "It's Piper." Pacing a few steps away she answered. "How is he?" The expression of desperate hope on her face fell almost immediately. "Yeah. Yeah, okay. Tell him I'll bring by some soup or a casserole or something. And to behave himself!" She hung up and addressed Nate. "It's definitely broken. He's in a cast for the next eight weeks."

"Looks like you're stuck with me," said Brody. It annoyed him that he felt as if he should apologize for that. He had just as much right to be here as she did.

"You'll make it work," said Nate, and it was as much faith as a direct order, judging by the look he shot them. "Now get back to places. Let's take it from the top."

"— JOLENE HELPS HIM USE that GPS app to track Mariah's phone, and she's down by the trail to the springs. So Larry goes out there, and what do you think she was doing out there in *broad day* at *high noon?*"

Tyler's eyes were peeled appropriately wide with anticipation as she continued to bag up her customer's purchase. "What?"

"Charlie Kingston! In a *car!* Can you imagine? Larry caught them *in flagrante*. I had it from Betsy Newman down at the police station that they nearly came to blows. Charlie's almost twice her age and *balding*. I just can't imagine what she thought she was doing."

Brody felt his lips twitch as he stepped up to the counter. "I expect she didn't realize discretion went the way of the dodo with the invention of smartphones."

"Why Brody Jensen, as I live and breathe. You come right over here and give me some sugar."

"Hi, Mrs. Landen," he said, leaning in to accept an exuberant squeeze from the woman who'd been his mother's partner in Bridge and Bitch for twenty years. He bussed her cheek. "You look wonderful. Great hair."

Mamie Landen beamed and patted the puffed up side ponytail of her improbably red hair. "Why thank you, darlin'. I'm embracing my inner Priscilla Presley today."

"Will that be cash or charge, Mrs. Landen?" Tyler asked.

Mamie dug in her voluminous handbag and produced a credit card. "So what brings you back to town? We haven't seen hide nor hair of you since your parents passed. God rest them. I know it must've been so hard for you to stay after the accident." She laid a hand on his arm and squeezed. She was the only one who'd cut him any slack for that. God love her.

"Thank you," Brody squeezed back, not missing the carefully blank look on Tyler's face as she continued to ring up the sale.

"Have you been out to see them yet?"

That right there. That was why he'd gone, why he'd sat and talked to a damned rock. So people would know he'd paid his respects as they expected. "A couple weeks ago." He hadn't been able to make himself go back again. He hadn't seen the need; his parents weren't there.

"I hope you found the site well-tended. Tyler makes sure to take fresh flowers every time she goes."

Distress and embarrassment flickered over Tyler's face before settling into resignation.

"The dahlias," Brody murmured, thinking of the bright pink blooms he'd found neatly arranged by the headstone. "They were you?"

She jerked one shoulder, staring at the receipt printing out rather than meeting his eyes. "I take them flowers when I go see Mom."

Every other week since her mother died of breast cancer back in high school, she took flowers to the gravesite. She found comfort and closeness there as he had not at his own parents' graves. But the idea of her showing that same dedication and devotion to them all this time made Brody's throat tighten. "That's really kind of you."

"You weren't the only one who lost them," she said softly.

No, he wasn't. Maybe he hadn't remembered that so much at the time. Tyler had been his rock, taking care of the details and picking up the shattered pieces of him after the accident. She was still taking care, even after all these years. Because they'd mattered to her. Because she knew the value of remembering.

Mamie stepped cheerfully into the awkward silence. "So you're here on the super secret project downtown. What's all that about?"

Brody struggled to pull himself back, to play the game social niceties dictated. "I'm surprised someone as well informed as you doesn't already know."

Her famous dimples flashed. "Well you *know* I was hoping for an inside scoop."

"No can do, Mrs. L. I am bound to secrecy." Brody softened the refusal with a smile he hoped came off as charming.

Undeterred, she turned back to Tyler and took the pen to sign her receipt. "Maybe you can weasel it out of him. Always could get this boy to do anything."

"Oh, he's better at keeping secrets than you might think. Thanks for stopping in today. And if you have any trouble with that pumpkin carving kit, you let me know. I also put in a handout with some websites that have patterns you can print off for free. It'd be a good project for y'all to do with the grandkids."

Brody recognized the redirect and noted Tyler's face fall out of the corner of his eye as Mamie stayed right where she was.

"I hear you two are headlining in *White Christmas*."

Brody nodded. "Alongside Piper Parish and Myles Stuart."

"It'll be so good to see the pair of you on stage again. Why, as soon as I heard, my Harold pulled out the DVD of that performance of *Oklahoma* so I could watch it again. Pure magic." Mamie clasped her hand over her heart and heaved a romantic sigh. "I can't wait to hear you sing again."

"Well you don't have to wait until December. Come by Speakeasy tonight, and you'll get your chance."

"Beg pardon?" Tyler asked.

"They're having a karaoke fundraiser for the theater. Nate canceled rehearsal for the night so the whole cast and a bunch of other past community theater performers can be there. People can pay to have any of us sing anything they want."

"Oh, what a marvelous idea! I'll be sure to be there. And I'll spread the word!"

She would, and it would be more effective than taking out an ad in the local paper, a highway billboard, and a TV commercial combined. With a cheerful wave, Mamie took her bag and left the shop.

"Why didn't anybody tell me about this?" Tyler's voice was just a shade too cool for polite.

"I'm telling you now. It was a last minute thing. Tucker's idea. He's taking the whole transition to Assistant Director a mite serious. You wanna ream somebody, ream him."

"I'm not gonna ream the injured guy."

"Then I guess you're singing. Assuming anybody picks you."

Her flat stare said volumes.

"Okay, yeah, of course they'll pick you. And me. And probably the pair of us. We can get over our crap and do this for a good cause."

"We're doing it for a pal in the Army," she muttered.

"Exactly," he grinned, leaning companionably against the counter.

"Sweetie, where do you want me to put this invoice for the—"

At the sound of the new voice, Brody straightened as if somebody had rammed a cattle prod up his ass. If he'd thought Tyler's look was chilly, the expression on her father's face was positively glacial.

"Jensen."

"Mr. Edison. Sir. Hello."

They stared at each other. Well. Mr. Edison glared and Brody looked back. The alternative was to haul ass with his tail between his legs and his pride wouldn't allow that. But what the hell did you say to a man, when the last time you saw him, you asked permission to marry his daughter? The same daughter who didn't want to marry you and was standing across the counter?

"Hey Dad," Tyler said—a little too cheerfully, Brody thought. "I didn't know you were back. Where's Ollie?"

Who's Ollie? he wondered.

Without shifting his gaze from Brody's, Sam Edison answered, "In the office having a snack. I'll take him home in a bit, but I wanted to drop off the progress report from the neurologist and a copy of the bill. Which is paid, by the way."

"Dad," Tyler chastised, "you don't need to do that."

"I'll do it if I want to, and you'll let me."

"Well, thank you." She moved out from the counter and pecked her father's cheek. Looking back, she asked, "Brody, did you need anything else?"

"No. Just delivering the message. So you'll be there?"

"I'll be there."

He lifted his hand in a wave, gave a curt nod to her father, and headed for the door as Tyler walked into the back office. As he pushed open the door, he saw her crouch down, saw the toys in the floor.

"Hey baby. Did you and Grandpa have a good day today?"

Brody nearly did a face plant as he stepped out onto the sidewalk. Tyler had a kid?

"ARE you sure you should be on your feet this much?" Tyler eyed Tucker as he crutched his way down Front Street toward Speakeasy Pizza.

"It's good practice on the crutches. Besides, another seven weeks and I'll be good as new. Doc said."

"Well, good. Then I only have to wait that long to kill you."

"Now why would you wanna go and do that?"

"Don't you dare play innocent, Tucker McGee. You knew exactly what you were doing when you set up this whole karaoke fundraiser."

"Bet your ass. The Madrigal's golden couple are both in town, both performing for the first time in years. I saw an opportunity, and I'm sure as hell exploiting it to raise bucks for the cause. Your names get butts in seats. That's the price of local fame, sugar, and I won't apologize for it. You've gotten over your shit with each other in rehearsal, you can do it for this."

Tyler scowled. That was true. Mostly. But a whole night of singing alongside Brody, where she knew with absolute certainty that some of the crowd would have them singing the love songs from the shows they were so known for, brought up feelings she didn't know how to deal with. Since she didn't have anywhere else to direct her ire, Tucker was a convenient target. "You waited 'til the last minute to have somebody tell me because you knew I wouldn't want to play. Sending Brody as your messenger really wasn't the smartest move you ever made."

Tucker paused on the sidewalk outside the pizzeria and sent her a smug smile. "You're here, aren't you?"

"Yes, damn you, I am. The one high point to all of this is that your Last Minute Man planning will keep it small scale." Tyler tugged open the door to Speakeasy and got blasted by a roar of sound.

"You were saying?" Tucker grinned and crutched through the door, past the hostess station, where Rachel Neely was taking the cover charge, and into the crowd.

Dear God, it's standing room only, Tyler thought, dazed as she followed him inside. A cheer went up at the sight of her. She shook hands, uttered greetings, and accepted enthusiastic high fives and fist bumps to the tune of applause. *Where did they all come from?*

Tucker made it to the stage first. Somebody gave him a mic. Evidently he was to be emcee for this shindig. "Hey there, everybody! Who's ready for some music?"

More cheers and claps. The rest of the cast, and a handful of other folks she'd acted with in the past, took up the tables in a semi-circle immediately by the little stage.

Tucker gestured to a marker board mounted on an easel beside the stage. "So here's how this is gonna work. We've got our performers listed in tiers. The more you love 'em, the more it'll cost to have them sing for you. The bottom tier will cost you five bucks per song per person. The top is pricier. Twenty bucks per song, per person. You want a duet, you get to pick who sings it and pay for the pair. Group stuff, same deal. We encourage you to pool your funds and remember that this is for a good cause, so don't be shy! You can pick anything in the book over here. We'll start off with a freebie to kick off the night. This one's for everybody." Tucker waved them all to the stage.

It was positively highway robbery. But as the group of them squished together on the stage, people lined up, cash and checkbooks in hand. At least half a dozen folks stuffed money in Tucker's jar as they kicked things off with a rousing rendition of "Any Way You Want It."

Brody flopped into a chair beside Tyler as Piper—one of the top tier singers—got drafted for "Diamonds Are A Girl's Best Friend." "He should be a snake oil salesman."

"Clearly," she agreed. "I can't believe people are paying money for this. And I can't believe how many people are *here.*"

"Might could've done with a change of venue. Ah, but the theater doesn't have pizza," he said, offering a smile to the waitress arriving with a tray.

"Large supreme, no mushrooms, due to the lady's allergy. You want another beer, Brody?"

He tipped his half-full bottle at the waitress. "Good on this, but maybe a couple pitchers of water with lemon. We're all gonna need them." The waitress left and Brody reached for a slice. "Dig in. No telling how long we'll be down before they call us again."

Tyler didn't move.

"What? Aren't you hungry?"

"You already ordered?"

"I knew you'd be getting off work later than most of the rest of us. Figured I'd have something pretty much ready when you got here so you could scarf between songs. Would you rather have something else?" He started to lift his hand to signal the waitress.

"No, no, this is fine. Thanks." He remembered her preference for pizza. He'd been *considerate. Points to him,* she thought, grabbing a piece.

Tyler got called up right after Piper for her first solo of the night on "Maybe This Time" from *Cabaret.* Somebody figured out how to operate the lights on the tiny stage and spotlit her for it. That made it easier, more like a real performance. The crowd kept them steadily busy with numbers from *Grease, Les Miserables,* and a handful of tunes from the early seasons of *Glee,* interspersed with Patsy Cline, Garth Brooks, and Carrie Underwood. She sang "Don't Go Breakin' My Heart" with Mitch, who'd been reluctantly drafted to the chorus for the show when Nate discovered he could move his feet. She made Ethel Merman proud as she dueled with Brody on "Anything You Can Do." And it wasn't weird. That made it easier to bring her A game and give the people what they wanted—and they wanted a lot. Tucker was making an effort to rotate through the singers, giving her and Brody a short break between numbers because, as he'd predicted, despite the price, they were the most popular choices.

She guzzled a glass of the lemon water, had another slice of pizza as her toes tapped to Tucker's rendition of "L-O-V-E."

"So what's the deal with Ollie?" Brody asked.

Tyler glanced at him. "What's what deal with Ollie?"

"Your dad said something about a neurologist?"

"Oh, that. About four months ago he had a—well the medical term is long and hard to pronounce, but basically a spinal stroke. It led to unilateral paralysis in his left side, so he's having to go through physical therapy and learn how to walk again."

"Jesus. That's horrible." He laid a hand over hers. "I'm really sorry you've had to go through that. Both of you. It must be really tough." The sincere concern on his face gave her pause.

"It hasn't been easy, but we're managing. His prognosis is good. The neurologist thinks he'll make an almost full recovery. But it'll be PT for several more months."

Tucker ended his number and signaled that she was up again. Tyler finished inhaling her slice and tossed back more water to wash it down.

"How old is he?"

"Seven," she said absently, heading for the stage.

As the opening bars of "It's All Coming Back To Me Now" began to play, she looked out at the audience and arched a brow. "Really?" Somebody cheered from the back of the room. Tyler just shook her head and offered up a little wave as she launched into the song. *Okay, fine. They want 1990s melodrama, I'll give it to them.* She hammed it up, wringing every ounce of parodied emotion out of the piece. She glanced at Brody, expecting to see him grinning in approval. But instead, his face was white, and he looked like he'd been sucker punched. What was that about?

When she finished, he met her at the edge of the stage to take the mic. Under the cover of applause, he said, "This is for you."

He was acting weird. The music started, and he fixed his gaze on her as he began to sing "I'll Stand By You."

Brody was a born performer. He had charisma dripping out his pores. But absolutely nothing paralleled his performances when he put the truth of himself into the music. It was that sincerity that *everyone* saw as he serenaded her from the stage. It was a song of promises. What business did he have singing this to her when he'd broken his so long ago?

Tyler felt her face flush and had to fight not to squirm in her seat.

The crowd went wild when he finished, a full-on standing ovation. Eyes still on her, he stepped off the stage, passing the mic off to Myles. Before the opening bars to the next song began, Tyler was out of her seat, jerking her head toward the fire exit and the alley.

As the door slapped shut behind him, Tyler turned on him. "Okay, what the hell was that? We've been singing together all night, and it wasn't weird. But you totally just made it weird."

Brody took her hands. "I mean it. Every word. I want to help."

Baffled, Tyler could only stare at him. "With what?"

"Ollie's medical bills for starters. Being a single parent is no joke, and even with your dad to help, it's got to be overwhelming. I'll do anything you need. Babysitting. Child support. I'd have been helping all this time, if only I'd known. Jesus, how could you not tell me, Tyler?"

He was so absolutely *earnest*. Tyler was pretty sure she'd been zapped to the *Twilight Zone.* Then what he'd said began to filter through her muddled brain, and she couldn't help it. She started to laugh.

"I hardly think this is a laughing matter." His stern expression only made her laugh harder at the utter ridiculousness of the situation.

"Brody, Ollie is my dog."

"Your…dog," he repeated. "But I heard you talking, at the shop earlier, saw the toys, and I thought…" He trailed off.

She made an effort to button down the giggles. "You thought he was my son. That he was *our* son."

"I…yeah."

The expression on his face sobered her right on up. The idea of it was so staggering, a dream of a future with him that she'd put away years ago.

Did he actually look crestfallen at the news that they *didn't* have a child together he didn't know about?

"Brody, honey, did you honestly think it was possible that I could've had a child, *your* child, and somehow you wouldn't have known about it? That I would have kept such a thing from you, if it were true?"

He released her to scrub both hands over his face. "Okay, yeah, when you put it that way, it does sound ridiculous. But I just... from what you said it sounded like you were talking to a child. And then he was seven. And..."

"You leapt to some really impressive conclusions." And with those conclusions, he'd immediately sought to do what he'd perceived as the right thing. She'd have to think about that later. "Why didn't you just ask outright? If not me, then Tucker or Piper. They could've told you otherwise."

"I figured if they hadn't told me, it was for a reason. Same with you. I... I'm sorry for making things weird. God, you must think I'm an idiot."

Tyler had thought him many things since his return. But this made her think he was sweet and a hell of a lot more adult than he'd been at twenty-one. Because she found she liked that about him, and because he looked really damned embarrassed now, she decided to cut him some slack. "Doesn't have to be weird if we don't let it be. Come on, I'm sure there's a list another mile long of requests waiting for us."

THE DOOR to Speakeasy closed behind them, abruptly cutting off the sound of voices and laughter, momentarily locking them into a cocoon of silence in the cold night. After the last several hours, it was glorious.

He'd opened the floodgates with his performance to Tyler. As soon as they stepped back inside, they got slammed with romantic duet requests. Anything and everything from their past roles, to jazz, to Garth Brooks and Tricia Yearwood. Various other members of the cast trickled out as the night wore on, but the crowd didn't thin. Not until Tucker had declared them off the roster—a good thing, as they were rapidly losing their voices —did the requests finally slow down. Over the course of the night, they'd fallen back into their rhythm. As he stood beside her, belting the final bars of "Come What May" from *Moulin Rouge,* he could almost let himself believe that they could find their way back to who they'd been together. God, he wanted to believe that.

Tyler paused and took a bracing breath, looking up at the clear sky.

"Where are you parked?" Brody asked.

"Back at the store."

Which was several blocks away. This was Wishful. She'd probably be fine that distance, but Brody had spent too much time in cities and was too much of a southern gentleman to let her walk it alone. "It's late. Let me walk you back to your truck." It was another small victory when she acquiesced without argument.

They fell into step, moving down the empty sidewalk in a silence that managed to be comfortable rather than awkward. That was a surprise, considering his earlier misconceptions about Ollie. Tyler had been amused and oddly understanding about the whole thing. He wondered if she was imagining, as he had been, that alternate reality where they made a family.

Shaking free of the image, he asked, "So you're working for your dad?"

Tyler shook her head. "He's retired. Not his idea, but he had a heart attack a few years back and doc said he had to slow down. I'm the boss these days. Since he *is* retired, he's been keeping Ollie for me while I'm working."

Running the family business wasn't what he'd expected of her. "Do you like it?"

She hummed a non-committal note. "I like working for myself. The nation-wide obsession with HGTV and home improvement means business has been pretty good, which hasn't been the case for a lot of mom and pop stores, so we're grateful for that. An Edison has run the shop for five generations. I couldn't be the one to change that."

Family ties. They ran deep for her. It was something he both admired and hated. Admired because of who that made her. Hated because he knew now that had been part of why she'd stayed rather than coming to him. But he wouldn't bring that up.

She jumped into the silence. "What about you? You're not working directly as a contractor anymore. Moved up the ranks, I take it."

"I'm a project manager," he said. "The one who juggles the contractors, engineers, and architects to make sure they all play nice and the project gets done on time and within budget."

"I guess the same memory skills you use for learning your lines come in handy for keeping up with that kind of detail."

"Doesn't hurt," he agreed. "You want to see the job site? It's just up that way." He gestured to the next block.

Her eyes sparkled. "Inside tour? Heck yeah. Everybody's buzzing about what they're putting in. Those in the know have been all hush hush."

"Gerald—my boss—had everybody who knows the particulars sign a non-disclosure agreement."

"Why?"

"For buzz. Not knowing makes people curious. Crazy curious. They can't stand a mystery."

"This is Wishful. There'd be buzz no matter what. You know that."

"Sure, but isn't a surprise more fun?"

Tyler tipped her head in acknowledgment of the point and waited while he pulled out his keys.

"I'm really quite impressed that the rumor mill hasn't sussed it out by now," he said. "I wouldn't have thought non-disclosure agreements would keep people from at least telling their spouses, who'd tell their friends—in confidence of course—who'd tell their friends, and so on."

"Oh, there's a pool on what it really is. I'm thought to have an inside track since the bulk of the materials have been purchased through us."

Brody pressed a hand to the small of her back and nudged her into the darkened building. "And what do you think it is?"

"Well, he's dropped a small fortune on high end bathroom fixtures, so my money is on hotel. There are also rumors about a spa. And a conference center. And Sally Forester said she gave him a tour of some other downtown property last week."

Brody switched on the flashlight app on his phone, holding it high.

"No electricity yet?" she asked.

"There is, but I'm not really supposed to be bringing you in here, so I don't wanna draw attention. C'mon." He grabbed her hand, tugged her along. "Watch your step."

Tyler dug her phone out, added its light to the cause as they walked. "So which is it? Or are you going to keep me in the dark despite this tantalizing preview?"

Brody paused and held out his pinky. "Do you solemnly swear not to reveal that which I tell to you tonight?"

"You're invoking the pinky swear?"

"Damn straight."

Grinning, she linked her finger with his. "I do so swear. Now spill it."

"Well, there are elements of truth to all of it. Hotel, spa, *and* conference facilities. Small ones anyway. He's wanting to provide some competition for the Alluvian." Located in Greenwood, right at the edge of the Mississippi Delta, the Alluvian was a high-end boutique hotel attached to a spa and the Viking Cooking School.

Tyler's eyes lit with interest. "*Really?* That *is* interesting. That kind of place will be a great draw for Wishful."

"Exactly. High end exec retreats. Bachelor and bachelorette parties. Romantic getaways," he said. "He's calling it the Babylon."

"Babylon, huh? Is that going to include hanging gardens?"

"Now you're getting the idea. On the roof. It'll be our own Wonder of the South when we're through. C'mon." He grabbed her hand again and pulled her through the ground floor of the space. "Dining room through there with a view opening up to the green and the fountain. Bar here. You can see they've already hung the pendant lights. Just waiting for the globes."

Tyler peeked under the protective contractor paper at the expanse of dark, glossy mahogany that made up the top of the bar. "Yeah, they've ordered some really fabulous swanky globes that, all together, amount to two months of mortgage payments. Should be in next week sometime."

"Front desk will be off to this side here. It's not been built yet, but you can see where it's roughed in." He tugged her up the wide expanse of the stairs. "Under all the paper, these are Cocobolo rosewood. Polished and gorgeous. And he's got a metalwork artist on tap designing the banisters out of wrought iron. Then up here we've got two floors of rooms, all named after Mississippi blues musicians."

"That's a nice touch. Let me guess, the swankiest of the swank is the B.B. King Suite?"

"You know it." Brody pulled her through the door, started gesturing. "A bed the size of an ocean liner will go there. A little sitting room there. Desk by the window. And through here is a tub you could swim laps in."

The tub itself had already been installed, as had the multi-head, glassed-in shower. It was this that Tyler made a beeline for, slipping through the glass door to turn a circle on the travertine tile. "God, I've had fantasies about this shower set up."

Brody was having one now, his brain more than happy to peel off all her clothes and turn on the water, until all that golden hair was plastered to her head and her curves were tantalizingly softened by billowing steam, such that he had to explore with his hands, his mouth…

She was looking at him, her eyes full of awareness in the dim light.

I could kiss her, he thought. *Just step in and back her up against the tiles.*

And then what? She wasn't just an itch to be scratched, no matter what kind of chemistry still flared between them. He was leaving in a matter of weeks.

He cleared his throat and shifted, squashing the fantasy that years hadn't passed and they weren't two different people now. "It's getting late. I should get you to your car."

Tyler said nothing on their way downstairs. The silence between them felt heavy with unsaid things. It stretched and grew as they made their way from the job site to the parking lot behind Edison Hardware and her truck. He waited quietly while she dug out the keys, opened the door and tossed in her purse.

"G'night then," he said.

"Good night," she said.

He started to turn away.

"Brody."

He shifted back to look at her, his heart beginning to thump.

But she said only, "Thanks for the tour," then slid into the truck and slammed the door between them.

6 WEEKS 'TIL SHOW

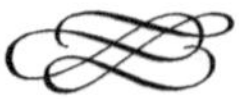

TYLER WAS NERVOUS.

SHE was never nervous.

But tonight... Tonight was the rehearsal of the cast party engagement scene. Tonight she'd kiss Brody. Kissing Tucker wouldn't have been a big deal. Like kissing her brother. Just exactly the kind of 1950s TV peck the role called for. She wouldn't *feel* anything kissing Tucker.

But Brody... There was too much history, too much *chemistry* between them. She'd seen it in his face that night at the hotel. Yet he hadn't acted on it. And part of her had been grateful for the fact that he hadn't pushed the issue and made her confront this.

Now, however, she'd have to confront it head on. With an audience. Awesome.

It would be fine. She would be fine. It was just a scene in a play. She was just a character. She popped a breath mint and stepped into the auditorium.

As if she were equipped with some kind of Brody-centric GPS system, her gaze zeroed in on him standing to the side of the orchestra pit, chatting with the strings section. Her heart leapt at the sight of him and her palms began to sweat.

I am so, so screwed.

"Our Judy has arrived, so let's get to this," Nate called.

"Showtime," Tyler muttered.

She dropped her bag into one of the front row seats and headed up the steps to her place on stage for the cast party scene. It began easily enough. There were lines to remember, dance moves, and lyrics. And then Piper-Betty went off in a snit and Myles-Bob stared after her in flustered confusion. It was time.

Tyler delivered her line invoking the announcement of the phony engagement, thinking, *Is this* really *absolutely necessary?*

Brody played his role, turning to their pianist and requesting his attention grabber. It was hard to remember that this was a part as he turned and called everyone's attention to them. Nerves skittered along Tyler's spine as all eyes turned to them. These were the same looks that had been following them for the last month since Brody walked back into Wishful and into her life. They all wanted to know how this was going to go down.

I am a professional, she told herself for the millionth time.

He announced the engagement. They hugged. Tyler was actually glad of Brody's arm around her because she wasn't quite sure she could stand steadily just now. Her smile felt brittle as congratulations and hugs were given. Piper-Betty squeezed her hard between delivering her lines. Tyler appreciated the support and wished she could make a swift exit stage-anywhere. As she turned to Brody, Piper seemed a little fiercer and more serious than necessary as she played the protective big sister, then made her exit to help Emma with champagne.

Tyler didn't hear the next lines. Not until their General Waverly piped up, "Well don't just stand there. Aren't you going to kiss the bride?"

And then Brody looked at her. "Oh! Yes, sir."

He swept in, dropped a quick, chaste peck, exactly as he was supposed to. But he didn't pull off the goofy, cheerful smile as he looked down at her, eyes going dark.

"Yes, sir," he said again—only this time, it was more of a growl.

All the air was promptly sucked out of the room. Brody framed her face, blocking her view of the others and ensuring her focus was only on him. As if she could possibly think of anyone else. One thumb brushed along the arch of her cheekbone in a caress that made her knees liquefy. His mouth settled over hers, warm and sure and desperately, deliciously familiar. Tyler didn't give a damn about the part, the performance. It took everything she had to hold herself still and non-reactive, waiting for him to finish.

But Brody didn't finish. He used his mouth to strip away every layer of her defenses with a brutal gentleness that left her wrecked and aching. Everything and everyone faded away except for him. He devastated her. Sliding right back into the chasm he'd left in her heart like a key into a lock. On a helpless, needy sound, she surrendered, damning herself and him as she ran her hands up his chest, into his hair and held on, as if sheer force of will would change the truth and hold him here as it hadn't before.

Cheers and wolf whistles broke out. She could feel Brody's lips curve, tasted his half-laugh before he eased back, and wanted to weep. With every inch, reality intruded. All these years, all the effort to put him out of her mind, out of her heart—undone with one kiss. Defenseless, she stared at Brody, waiting for her system to level. But her heart continued to pound, her stomach twisting into slippery knots. Something hot and hard lodged behind her breastbone, and she couldn't quite breathe past it.

What have I done?

"That wasn't so bad, was it?" he whispered.

The tears spilled over, hot and fast. Mortified, Tyler shoved away from him, stumbling back. "I'm sorry. I can't do this."

"Tyler—"

She had vague impressions of shock, concern.

Out, out. I have to get out.

Piper stepped toward her, but Tyler spun away, desperate to escape. "I can't do this," she repeated. And she ran.

Shit!

Brody's head spun, his world-class balance shaken. He'd gone well beyond what was called for by the part. Not on purpose, but at his first taste, he'd fallen into the kiss, into her. So he'd gone with it, pouring out everything he felt, everything he couldn't say, because he realized he would never get enough of this woman. Brody expected to see heat in her eyes—temper and lust in equal measure. And maybe, after how she'd kissed him back, something of the way she used to look at him. But she'd looked...utterly devastated. She'd *cried.* He was caught somewhere between shock and feeling like ten kinds of ass as she made a running exit stage left.

What the hell just happened?

The backstage door banged open as she hit the metal bar and kept going. The sound echoed through the cavernous space like a gunshot and jarred him into action. Brody made it to the door before it had relatched, slamming into the alley behind the theater. There was only one way she could go, so he took off at a sprint. He burst out on Front Street and veered to the right, knowing instinctively she'd head for the fountain on the green. She was already two blocks ahead.

God, he'd forgotten how fast she was.

"Tyler!"

She poured on the speed that had won countless track meets in high school, as if she was running from hell hounds instead of him. And that just added a layer of pissed off to the confusion and concern. Brody lengthened his stride, long legs eating up the distance between them. Tyler darted across Main Street and into the park. He raced after her, narrowly avoiding being clipped by an SUV that laid on the horn and swerved with a squeal of tires.

Tyler skidded to a halt and whirled at the sound. But the fear on her face vanished as he cornered her.

"Leave me alone."

"Not a chance. You've never walked out of a rehearsal in your life. What the hell happened back there?" he demanded.

Somewhere during her escape, she'd stopped crying and found a thread of temper. Color rode high in her cheeks and her eyes sparked as she glared at him. Thank God for it. He could deal with anger and relished the idea of a fight to clear the air.

"Why couldn't you just stay away? Why did you have to come back here and ruin everything?"

What kind of alternate reality had he landed in? "Why are you pissed at me, Tyler? It was your decision."

She gaped at him. "What was my decision? You *left,* Brody."

"Yes, I left. And you didn't follow."

"How was I supposed to follow? You didn't say a word. Not where you were going, not why, not goodbye. God, I worried myself sick for months before *somebody* caught wind that you hadn't died in a ditch somewhere. And I got it. I got that it hurt to stay here after your folks died. I got that you needed space to figure things out. But did you have to be so cruel about it? You could not possibly have made it more abundantly clear that Wishful wasn't enough for you. That *I* wasn't enough for you."

It was his turn to gape. "I waited for you to come to me in Paris."

"Paris? What are you talking about?"

"I sent you a plane ticket. And instructions for you to meet me at the top of the Eiffel Tower." He'd waited there, in the whipping wind, ring burning a hole in his pocket all day and into the night, until they'd kicked him out because they were shutting down the elevator until the next day.

"When?"

"Right before I left town. I put it in the mail drop at the Grind and went to the airport. I thought you'd be right behind me."

Tyler stared.

"You never got it." It wasn't a question. Not with that shattered expression on her face. A pit opened in his stomach, full of dawning dread.

"Dave Lautner took out the mail drop when he plowed into the front of the coffee shop. It happened the day you left."

Brody thought of the handsome patio seating and changed entrance. The plane ticket tied to his future had been destroyed in a freak accident, and he'd been too goddamned pig-headed to follow up when she hadn't come. *Jesus H. Christ, I'm an idiot.* Brody closed his eyes.

"I thought when you didn't come," he said quietly, "it was your way of saying you didn't want to be with me. That I was too damaged for you after everything that had happened. I know how much you hate confrontations."

Tyler sputtered with incredulity. "Mail gets lost all the time. Why didn't you call or write…*something?*"

"I…was hurt and angry and so, so completely stupid."

Eight years. I wasted eight years and lost her over my damned fool pride.

Brody waited for recriminations. Because, yeah, this was entirely his fault. He'd cut ties and never looked back, never asked for an explanation, never pulled his head out of his ass to confront her. But there was something else in her face as she looked up at him.

A fragile hope.

"You wanted me to come with you?" she whispered.

He didn't touch her. He was too afraid she might break. But the answer came easily. "Always."

"All these years," she murmured, arms wrapping around her middle. "All these years, I wondered what I'd done to make you stop loving me."

The stark pain on her face made him bleed. He said her name, and he didn't know if it was apology or plea because the tears were slipping down her cheeks again. "I never stopped loving you. Ever."

She laid a hand over her heart and rubbed. "I don't know if that's wonderful or heart-breaking. Eight years, Brody. I've spent twice as long as we were together believing the absolute worst of you, doing everything in my power not to love you. How can I feel this much, when it's been eight years?" she demanded.

Hope lit inside him like a rocket. Because he couldn't stand it anymore, he reached for her, gratified when she hesitated only a moment before burrowing in and holding on.

Don't let go, he thought. *Don't ever let go again.*

They stood like that beside the fountain, until her tears stopped and the tension bled out of her shoulders. Lifting her wet face, Tyler studied him, frowning. "I don't know what to do with all the feelings you stir up in me."

Brody stroked the length of her back, soothing both of them. "You don't have to do anything with them right this second."

"We have to talk about this."

"And we will. Later." He brushed away her tears. "Right now, you need to pull yourself together, and we need to go back to rehearsal."

Her mouth dropped open. "You can't be serious."

"If you don't go back and face everyone now, it'll be that much worse at the next rehearsal. And there *will* be a next rehearsal because you can't and won't let the Madrigal down."

She winced and swiped at the tears on her cheeks. "You're right. You're right. I really *hate* that."

"No one's going to hold it against you. No matter how much it looks like they welcomed me back, I'm still the outsider here. They're all on your side. And I'm pretty sure from the look she shot me when I left, Piper may be planning to string me up by the balls."

"That would be merciful compared to some of what we planned at the time."

"Yeesh." He made an exaggerated pained expression to try and tease a smile out of her as she stepped back. He only got one corner of her mouth to lift.

"Tyler, I am sorry I hurt you. That I hurt us."

She glanced up at him with unreadable eyes. "So am I."

READY OR NOT, Tyler thought, tugging open the auditorium door. She'd stopped in the lobby restroom to wash her face, but that was just delaying the inevitable. Any hope she'd entertained that they'd shifted scenes to rehearse something else was dashed as all talking came to a screeching halt and all eyes turned to her. Tyler froze in the sticky silence, knowing she'd been the topic of their conversation. This wasn't at all like being the center of attention on stage for a show. This was her life.

Brody stepped up behind her, pressing a hand to the small of her back. Part comfort, part nudge. The touch made her pulse leap and her chest tighten.

I never stopped loving you. Ever.

His words echoed through her mind, mending something long broken inside. How could she think, how could she act, with *that* hanging unresolved between them?

"I'm right here with you," he murmured, and his breath tickled her ear, stirring something considerably lower.

The sooner I face them, the sooner this rehearsal is over, and the sooner we can talk about this. Though talking wasn't exactly her body's preferred first order of business at the moment. Tyler straightened her spine—and still she couldn't move.

Brody stepped beside her and held out a hand. She eyed it, knowing that taking it would be the best thing for the show, would put the rest of the cast at ease and prove that she and Brody could work together. But she couldn't help feeling he wasn't thinking about any of that. His gaze was steady on her, ignoring everyone else, and Tyler understood he wasn't asking about facing the cast or doing the show. Could she really bridge the gap of those eight years, give him another chance?

Don't think about the past or the future. Just focus on the now.

She laid her hand in his. His fingers curled sure and solid around hers, and it felt...right.

They made their way down the aisle, up to the edge of the stage. Because she still wanted to mumble, Tyler lifted her chin and her voice until everyone could hear. "I apologize for the disruption. I'm ready to get back to rehearsal now."

"Well, everyone is allowed one diva moment per show." Nate gave her a long, measured look. "Except you, Myles."

Myles affected a crestfallen expression and everyone laughed. The tension level dropped perceptibly.

As they made their way back to their places onstage, Nate continued, "Just to be clear, it's *Betty* who hurries off and *Bob* who chases after her. And Brody, remember this is *White Christmas*, not *Basic Instinct.*"

"I'd pay money to see that," muttered a woman on the back row.

Tyler felt her face flame.

Brody's lips twitched. "My mistake."

Nate clapped his hands and turned back to the assembled cast. "Okay people, let's pick up where we left off. After the kiss."

They ran the scene. Mistakes were made, but none so major as to necessitate a second run. They had time yet for that, and Tyler knew Nate was cutting her a break. As soon as they wrapped for the night, Piper made a beeline for the front row seat where they'd left their bags.

"Are you all right?"

Sensing eyes on her, Tyler looked across the auditorium to where Tucker had cornered Brody. The punch of Brody's gaze made her pulse leap, but she wasn't entirely sure if it was fear or anticipation.

I never stopped loving you. Ever.

"I don't know what I am."

"Do you want me to come over? There's emergency Ben and Jerry's in my freezer. It wouldn't take me ten minutes to swing by and pick it up."

Tyler shifted her attention fully to Piper and mustered a smile. "No, that's not necessary. Brody and I have a conversation to finish. It may take a while. You go on home."

"A conversation," she repeated. "About that kiss?"

"And what happened eight years ago. We need to clear the air if we're going to finish the show together, and neither of us wants to let the Madrigal down. I'll be fine."

Skepticism and worry warred on Piper's expressive face. She leaned in for a quick, fierce hug. "Whatever way it goes, if you need to, call me after. Or come over. I don't care what time it is."

Tyler knew she wouldn't do either, but she appreciated the offer.

Everybody filed out, including Nate.

Brody walked over, a keyring in hand. "I said we'd turn off lights and lock up. You good to talk?"

"Yeah. It's after ten. Dad and I have an arrangement that if I don't get Ollie by then, he stays overnight."

The last door fell shut with an echo. In the silence, she heard the softer click of the lobby door shutting behind her castmates, leaving her alone with the man who'd ripped her heart out, all because of his idiotic, stubborn pride. They'd fallen in love in this theater, on this stage. It seemed fitting that the next phase of... whatever they would become should begin here.

Tyler wandered back on stage and sat at the edge, legs dangling into the orchestra pit, while the old building popped and groaned like a grumpy old woman, settling around them for the night.

He smiled at her. "I imagined you here, over the years. Wondering what roles you played."

"None. This is the first show I've been in since you left."

That seemed to surprise him. "Why?" he asked.

"My heart had gone out of it. I couldn't fathom performing across from anyone else. It seemed best to hang up my dancing shoes and put them away with other childish things."

"We were hardly children," said Brody, settling beside her. He was close, but not touching her.

"No, but our romance was the stuff of fairy tales and dreams. And then you left and I woke up to the reality of a life without you."

"Tyler—"

"No, let me finish. When I saw your name on that cast list, I was furious. Absolutely livid that you had the gall to come back, to audition, now, when I'd spent *years* making my way on my own. Because it didn't matter if it was eight years or eight days. The hurt was still fresh. Knowing the why behind your actions mitigates that some, but it just makes me sad and angry for a whole different set of reasons."

"You have every reason to feel that way. I screwed up." That he owned it helped, just a little.

"You did," she agreed. "After you left, a lot of people thought you blamed yourself for your parents' death. You were messed up and hurting. And they thought your leaving was some kind of admission of guilt. After a couple years, I stopped defending you because I couldn't make sense of what you'd done either, and I was tired of all the looks of pity."

"God, no wonder people gave me the cold shoulder."

"I'm not here to beat you up over it. I find that, faced with the truth of what really happened, it'd be like beating a dead horse. We've both been punished enough."

"What exactly are you saying?"

God, there was no way she could look at him. Instead, she

looked at their hands, each curled around the worn wooden edge of the stage, separated by a couple of inches that were filled with years.

"I think you proved beyond a reasonable doubt that we still have chemistry. We always did, so that's not much of a surprise. But I need to know—or maybe I need clarification of what you meant by what you said earlier." Her chest felt tight, and Tyler found she couldn't quite take a full breath as she waited for his reply.

"All right. Fair enough. You've said your piece, now I'm gonna say mine. I know we've got chemistry. I knew it the moment I saw you again, and I'll admit that I shamelessly exploited that on stage tonight. I know all your buttons, and I pushed them with the intent to get a reaction, to make you remember how good we are together. Seeing as we both finally got the truth out of it, I can't say I mind the end result. But I know I stirred you up, and I'll understand if whatever you're feeling is…residual from what we were before. It doesn't feel residual for me, though. Not from the moment I saw you again."

A painful sort of hope lit inside her. But she'd been through far too much to leap at a whim. "The fact is, Brody, you don't know me anymore. I'm not the girl you left behind, and you're not the boy who walked away."

"Bullshit. You haven't changed that much."

Impatience simmered because she recognized that she was going to have to be the voice of reason here. "You don't *know* that. You *don't,*" she repeated when he started to speak. "Do I feel something for you? I'd be lying if I said I didn't. But I don't know if it's real or just remnants of what came before that never got resolved. I can't answer that question."

"Isn't it worth finding out?"

Tyler studied his face, memorizing the lines and curves, noting how he'd changed, how he was the same. Tipping forward she brushed her lips over his, just because she could, because she ached for the taste of him. She knew that the sensible thing was to let him go, take this truth and whatever peace it brokered between them, and shut the door on the past.

I never stopped loving you. Ever.

Tyler fisted her hand in his shirt and let the whip of need lash through her. So long. So damned long. God, didn't they deserve *something*? For a moment, she wavered, beyond tempted to be reckless, to take the heat they brought each other and ride it to whatever glorious end they could.

But she'd been left in the ashes before.

Heart still thundering, she flattened her palm and eased back, resting her temple against his.

"That felt pretty damned current to me." The rasp of Brody's voice stroked over her like a caress.

Uncertain whether her voice would work, Tyler made a noncommittal hum.

"We have something between us, Tyler. We always did."

She couldn't deny that and didn't try. "Brody, I can't just…fall back into this." *Yes, I absolutely could,* she thought, *with very little provocation.* She wanted this, wanted him, on whatever terms she could get. But she had to be sensible. She had to think about tomorrow.

"I get it. I respect that. But just…" He cupped her cheek and Tyler cursed herself, even as she leaned into the touch. "Think about it."

"Okay," she agreed.

Brody's gaze slid down to her mouth, his eyes going dark. Tyler felt her pulse jump again, started to sway toward him. He slid off the stage, down to the floor and turned to reach for her. Because she was still short of breath, Tyler let him help her down, let him hold her until she steadied.

"Okay," she said again.

"Let me walk you to your truck."

5 WEEKS 'TIL SHOW

CROSS THE STAGE, GENERAL Waverly stood, menus in hand, while Bob, Phil, and the Haynes sisters dined and discussed how to help him. Just as Bob rose to go place the call to bring the show to Pine Tree, a long, low groan echoed through the theater.

"What the hell was that?" Piper asked, stepping fully out of character.

"Obviously it's the ghost of old Mr. Stanton himself opining about how that scene was running," Nate said, "which was terrible. Brody, if you could take your eyes off Tyler for five seconds and actually play your part, we'd all appreciate it."

Tyler looked over at him, startled, a pretty pink flush creeping across her cheeks. Brody could only grin at her. No sense in pretending remorse he didn't feel. But he saluted the director. "Yes, boss."

"Again, from the top."

Brody took his position, started the scene over. He did his best to stay in character, to look where he was supposed to look, say what he was supposed to say. But his mind was full of Tyler.

In the week since they'd broken their stalemate, he'd made

excuses to see her. He took over the daily supply run for the hotel job just for the chance to make her smile at the start of the day. And it had been a simple matter to start taking his lunch breaks when she did, either eating take out at the store or over at Dinner Belles, where they shared a slice of Mama Pearl's pie. That they could share a meal and a joke, without that angry tension hovering between them was a minor miracle. Though there'd been no more of those blistering kisses, she was spending time with him, willingly, without trying to push him away. It was progress, and that should've been enough for him.

But it wasn't.

Time was galloping by, and each workday brought a reminder of the end of the job and the start of the next, which would take him away from Wishful, away from Tyler. He didn't bring it up, knowing that would hardly help his case. At least half of her caution was wrapped up in the brevity of their time together. But urgency nipped at his heels, urging him to push, to demand.

He'd promised he wouldn't. She wanted to take things slow and easy so she could figure things out, and Brody respected that. But what was there to figure out? They practically combusted when they got within three feet of each other. For all that she said he didn't know her anymore, he hadn't seen anything that made him love her any less.

Patience is a virtue, Jensen, he reminded himself. Albeit not one he'd ever been blessed with, particularly when it came to one Tyler Edison.

A sense of relief and anticipation flooded through him at the opening bars to "Mandy." Keeping his promise not to push had meant keeping his hands to himself. But all bets were off when they danced. His eyes followed her as she made her way down the risers, dancing and flirting past all the guys on the cast. She was glorious. Lithe and charismatic in a way that had every set of eyes centered on her. At the bottom of the stairs, she linked arms with him and Myles for the easy tap portion of the number, which

Myles pulled off with more aplomb than he'd managed on the previous run. And at last the cue came and Brody took Tyler's hand, spinning her into his arms for the complicated part of the routine.

Her eyes sparked and her smile spread. Brody lost himself—in the music, in her, in the unique intimacy they shared while dancing. She arched back over his knee, pointing one long leg high into the air in a manner that had him thinking all about other uses for her miraculous flexibility. She moved with him, responsive to every touch, every step, fully in sync. Heat and awareness flared between them. The pace of the music picked up and they danced their way through the pack, and up the risers for the finale of the song, where she ended, perched on his shoulder.

"Finally, something went right!" Nate cheered.

Tyler's hands curled around Brody's forearms, as he slid her down the length of his body. The pulse at her throat beat like a hummingbird's wings, and her chest rose and fell against his as she worked to catch her breath. Brody didn't release her when her feet hit the step, and she made no effort to move away, instead staring up at him with dark, hungry eyes.

"Well this is going to be the hottest Christmas to date," Myles whispered.

"Pretty sure that's the most provocative version of that song ever done," someone else added.

Abruptly conscious of their audience, Brody ran his hands from Tyler's shoulders to her waist, squeezing once before setting her away from him. The long groan came again. The theater offering up sympathy for his frustrated libido, no doubt.

"The next scene requires some set changes," Nate said. "Let's take care of that and pick up there tomorrow night."

The set change burned off a little of the energy humming in Brody's blood, giving him something else to focus on besides the remembered feel of Tyler's body flush against his. At least until he caught her looking at him from across the stage as Nate made his end-of-rehearsal announcements. As soon as rehearsal wrapped, he gathered his gear and met Tyler at the head of the aisle to walk out.

"Good rehearsal tonight," he said.

"For one of us anyway," she grinned. "Nate's gonna kill you if you don't focus."

"You could help me with that, you know. We could go get a drink or a late supper. Discuss the possibility of running lines."

Tyler slanted him a glance, one corner of that luscious mouth lifting in delighted amusement. "Right. I remember exactly what you used to call running lines."

Brody swung an arm around her shoulders and bent to whisper in her ear, "I've still got the old sofa of my parents where we used to do that. We could—"

The groan came again, bigger, louder this time, rising to a shriek above them. As the ceiling above began to cave, Brody shouted, "Move!" He swung around and dove backward, landing hard on Tyler as a huge portion of the mezzanine balcony collapsed behind them. Debris rained over them both. Brody curled his body over Tyler's, taking the brunt of the impact.

In the wake of the crash, the silence was deafening. Brody lifted his head, squinting through the dust to see people running toward them down the aisles. He rolled to the side, hauling himself into a kneeling position beside Tyler. Her face was white. "Are you all right?" he demanded. He didn't wait for her response, already running his hands over her limbs, checking for breaks and abrasions.

"I'm fine." She coughed. "You just knocked the wind out of me."

"Somebody go out the side door, check to make sure everybody made it into the lobby," Tucker ordered from somewhere behind them.

A quick search and head count assured them that no one had been caught in the collapse.

"Thank God," Tyler breathed. When she reached for him, Brody pulled her close. "You kept me from becoming a pancake."

"I guess all those noises weren't old Mr. Stanton after all," Piper said.

Nate laced his hands behind his head and stared at the central section of the balcony, now blocking the auditorium doors. "This is a disaster."

"The important thing is that no one was hurt," Barbara Monahan began.

"We can't have a show in a theater that's falling apart. There's barely money to put on the show. We don't have the kind of time *or* money to get this fixed, and Stanton's kids aren't going to shell out for this," said Nate.

The air of defeat settled over them like lead.

"It's over," Nate declared.

Brody looked down at Tyler, all thoughts of lust and flirtation forgotten. Distress was etched across her features.

"The fat lady hasn't sung yet," he said. "The show will go on." But despite his conviction, as he stared at the rubble, he knew they were gonna need a miracle.

"I FEEL like there should be pizza for a summit meeting," Tucker pronounced.

"It's too early for pizza," Piper said.

"It's never too early for pizza."

"Either way, it's hard to have a summit meeting when not everybody is here yet," Piper pointed out.

"Brody hasn't quite shaken loose of work yet, and Norah should be getting out of her meeting with the mayor shortly." Tyler paced restlessly in front of the register. The store was bless-edly empty at the moment but for her friends, who crowded around the table in the consult area. She'd have been hard pressed to offer up the requisite customer service.

"How are things going with Brody?" Piper asked.

Tyler wasn't fooled by the über casual tone of her voice. "They're…going." She'd promised Brody she'd think about what was between them. In truth, she'd thought of little else. Things had been so good the last week—familiar, comfortable in their common purpose. It would be easy, so very easy, to let herself fall back into love, back into a relationship with him. But a part of her was still waiting for him to leave, counting down the days to the end of the year when the hotel job was finished. It was the elephant in the room they continued to stubbornly avoid, all as part of their efforts to pretend they had time to ease back into things—just like Tyler had requested.

Unfortunately, that elephant was getting harder and harder for her to ignore.

Piper was prevented from prying further by the arrival of Brody himself. "Sorry I'm late. I had to juggle some stuff to get free, and then Gerald called wanting an update. Any news?"

"None yet. The engineers turned in their reports. Norah's in with the mayor." Tyler paced another lap.

"You're gonna wear a hole in that floor." Brody stepped into her path and rubbed his hands up and down the length of her arms.

"I can't settle," she said.

"It'll be okay. C'mon. Sit down."

Tyler didn't want to sit and certainly didn't think it would be okay. But she let him draw her to the table. Before her butt even hit the seat of a chair, the shop bell jangled as Norah strode in. Tyler shot to her feet. "Well?" she demanded.

"It's bad," Norah said. "Like, closed unless repairs can be made kind of bad. I'm afraid we're done, y'all."

The news was met with a chorus of groans and expletives as everyone began to talk over each other.

Tyler's shoulders slumped under the weight of disappointment. She hadn't realized how much the Madrigal meant to her until faced with the prospect of losing it. And now...now it was over. It felt like an ending of far more than the show. It was the end of an era. A closed chapter in Wishful's history and her own. She'd never again get the chance to perform on that stage.

Brody slipped an arm around her. Grief twisted through her, a knife in her chest. With the Madrigal gone, she'd never get the chance to perform with him again. Never fall in love through someone else's story. Leaning into his embrace, Tyler knew the heartache was as much about Brody as the theater. The demise of the place that had given them hope of starting over felt like an ominous sign for their future.

"Do you have the report from the structural engineer?" Brody asked.

Norah dug a folder out of her purse and offered it to him. With a quick squeeze, he let Tyler go and reached for it.

"I don't know what we could possibly do," Tucker said. "It's five weeks 'til the show. I hate to be a downer, but that's not much time for anything."

"We could try to find another venue," Piper suggested.

"Where?" Tyler asked. "None of the churches have space enough for a set of that size. Maybe the high school gym, but it's not a stage. I don't know how any of the set changes would work, and there's no structure for the backdrops or lighting."

"What about the community center?" Norah offered.

"Same deal as the school gym," Tyler said.

"The fact is, this whole campaign was to save the theater from financial ruin," Tucker pointed out. "If there are structural problems on top of everything else, that kind of money's so far above and beyond what we could pull off." He shook his head.

"I can fix it," Brody said.

Conversation ground to a halt. All attention shifted to him.

Tyler stared at him. "What?"

"I think this can be salvaged," he said, looking up from the report in his hands.

"Bro, we need way more than 'salvaged'," Tucker said.

But Tyler's heart was already thumping with a spurt of hope.

"No, listen," Brody insisted. "I know it looks bad, but the main building is structurally intact. It's the integrity of the balcony that's in question. If we clear out the debris, shore up the supports of the sections remaining so that they pass code, then we could still pull off the show."

"Yeah, us and what army?" Piper asked.

"In case you've forgotten, I am a licensed contractor."

"That's great, but you're one guy," Piper argued. "Even with volunteers, we don't have enough trained labor to pull off something like this."

Brody laid the folder on the table and crossed his arms. Tyler immediately recognized the stubborn jut to his chin. "I have an entire crew. We're way ahead on the downtown job, to the point that we're actually waiting on some deliveries before we can keep moving forward. I can pull them, put them over at the theater."

"There's still the matter of the money, boy-o," Tucker said. "We can't pay them."

"A bunch of them would volunteer, and we can pull in others from the community."

"I know several who would help," Tyler added, warming to the idea, her mind already spinning, filling with names.

"Even with labor, I doubt the three grand we made from karaoke night is going to cover even the materials for repairs of this magnitude."

"Hello," Tyler waved. "I own a building supply store. I'll donate what I can, and we can put the karaoke funds toward any specialized materials we need."

"And whatever that doesn't cover, I will," Brody said.

Everyone gaped at him.

"I...Brody, that's potentially no small chunk of change," Tyler breathed.

He jerked one shoulder in a shrug, his eyes fixed on hers. "I've done very well for myself. And it's worth every penny to me for the chance to preserve a piece of our history."

Our history. Not the town's. There could be no mistaking that with the look in his eyes. He meant to save the place where they'd fallen in love. This was important to him. *She* was important to him.

Tyler felt her heart do a slow roll in her chest.

Swallowing against the words that clogged her throat, she reached up to cup his face. Stubble rasped against her fingers as she leaned in and laid her lips softly over his.

"Thank you," she whispered.

"For what?"

"For trying."

His lips curved into a grin. "If I get that for trying, what do I get for pulling it off?"

Tyler laughed. "Do it and find out." She started to pull back, but he caught her around the waist.

"I think you'll find that I'm very serious and very committed to restoration."

Slowly, she nodded. "I think you are."

At the sound of a sigh, Tyler eased back. Norah clutched a hand over her heart, wearing the same sappy smile Tyler had reason to know she wore at the end of all good chick flicks. Tucker was smirking, and Piper watched them with an expression she couldn't read.

I've really got to stop doing this stuff with an audience.

She cleared her throat. "So. We have a plan for labor and materials. We'll need to get in and do a more thorough evaluation of the specifics of what will be needed on both fronts. I'll start getting in touch with people to ask about volunteer labor."

"What about the permits?" Piper asked. "Aren't those required for this kind of work?"

"I can push those through," Norah said.

"This whole plan presupposes that the Stantons will even let us do this," Tucker said. "You can't exactly do construction on a building you don't own without permission."

Tyler bristled. "What is *wrong* with you? When did you turn into a pessimist about this project?"

"About the time the balcony came crashing down. I'm not saying we shouldn't try. Just trying to point out the road-blocks before we get into things and waste time, money, and effort on something that can't be followed through."

Brody tugged Tyler closer, until her back pressed against his chest. "No, he's right to bring it up. We have to manage all the details if we're going to pull this off."

Norah grinned, in her element. "Have faith and leave them to me."

∼

IT ALWAYS LOOKS WORSE *before it looks better,* Brody reminded himself. And it did look bad right now.

The debris had been fully cleared away. The remaining segments of the balcony were jacked up and rigged with tempo-rary supports. The seats they were able to salvage had been detached and relocated for cleaning, along with several sections that had to be removed for equipment access. A hole gaped in the center, reminding him of a fighter down his two front teeth. Which wasn't a bad analogy, actually, as this whole thing felt like a sucker punch. Much like finding out how things had gone so horribly wrong with Tyler all those years ago.

"We'll fix you up, old girl," Brody murmured. "And maybe it'll be enough to change her mind." He didn't know how to fix things with Tyler, or how things would work out between them in the end. But making the repairs on the theater was solidly in his wheelhouse, so, for now, the focus had to be on the job. He couldn't let himself think beyond that.

The emergency exit opened on a shriek of hinges. Roy Simmons, one of the carpenters from the Babylon job, poked his head in. "Supply truck is here."

Shaking himself out of his musings, Brody waved in acknowledgment. *Time to get this show on the road.*

He headed to the front of the building. The carpeted lobby was covered in drop cloths, and a handful of men were setting up work stations near the available electrical outlets. Outside, beyond the dumpster that had been hauled in for demolition, a large flatbed truck with the Edison Hardware logo emblazoned on the door, was parked at the curb. Tyler slid out of the driver's seat as he emerged. Her hair was drawn back into a pony tail, pulled through the back of a maroon MSU baseball cap. In work-worn jeans with frayed hems and a black track jacket to ward off the chill of early morning, she looked mouth-watering.

"You're amazingly bright-eyed considering the hour." Brody crossed to her.

She ducked back into the cab and came out with a pair of extra tall to-go cups. "I've already been by the Grind."

He took the one she offered him and sipped. His eyebrows shot up at the first, rich punch of sweetened coffee. "Jesus, no wonder you're awake. What is this, a triple-shot espresso?"

"They're calling it the Zombie Killer these days. Hey, it worked for finals week in college. It'll work for this. There are donuts in the truck for everybody. How many folks did we end up with today?"

"Ten signed up for this shift, besides me. Mitch is leading up the second crew that's coming on for the night shift. Not sure of the final count for them, but similar numbers." They'd have more when it came to reassembling the final touches, but for now, it was all skilled labor, divided into two crews on a schedule that would rival those on the set of any HGTV crash renovation.

"Then I'll make an even dozen," she said.

"You don't have to work?"

"Dad's covering the store the rest of this week so I can help out."

Brody rearranged details and work crews in his mind to accommodate the extra hands. They'd need every pair they could get. "Been a long time since we swung hammers together." It had been a long time since he'd picked up a hammer at all. He was too used to overseeing, managing jobs from the top down. This was his first opportunity to really run a crew in several years, and he found himself itching to get started.

"I'm still in practice." Tyler reached back into the truck and drew out a tool belt. She set the coffee down and snapped it on.

Brody took another swig of coffee to wet his suddenly dry mouth. "You look entirely too good in that thing." The whole picture was that much hotter knowing she was more than capable with all the tools attached to it.

Tyler just smiled. "Let's get this stuff unloaded. Where do you want it?"

By the time the materials were unloaded, the remainder of the crew had arrived. Gathering around the blueprints he'd drawn up and printed last night, the team listened as Brody laid out the plan of attack. It felt good to have his hands back in design, to figure out what could be salvaged and how the details could be tied back to the original concept. The end result wouldn't be seamless—not on the schedule they were running—but it would be functional and, more to the point, safe. That would buy them time to save the theater by their original plan. And then...well, they'd see what happened.

"Okay, so everybody's got their work assignments. Any questions?" A hand shot up in the back. "Yes, Paul?"

"You sure you still remember how to do this? I can't remember the last time you picked up anything heavier than a pencil." Paul's mouth twitched. They'd worked together on jobs from coast to coast over the last five years, with Paul preferring to keep his hands directly on the pulse of the projects, even as Brody climbed the management ladder.

Brody cupped his ear. "Methinks I hear a challenge."

"Calling it like I see it, Jensen."

"Before either of you hauls off to prove your manhood," Tyler interjected. "I feel compelled to point out that you aren't lumberjacks and you won't be chopping down trees."

Paul made a sound of mock disappointment. "And what will you be doing, little lady? Making sandwiches? I notice Brody didn't include you in the work assignments."

Brody braced himself, waiting for Tyler to pop off, as she'd been wont to do back in the day when those on a job insulted her abilities.

She cut her eyes toward him, and he caught the glint of amusement as her lips curved into a sweet smile. "I'll be making that router table and table saw sing sweet, sweet hymns to match the vintage, custom moulding."

Paul blinked. A few of the local men, who knew Tyler, chuckled.

Brody crossed his arms. "Tyler's fifth generation of a lumber family and the owner of our biggest supplier. There's nothing she can't do with wood." Someone choked on a laugh. If any of them thought of offering up some rejoinder to that vaguely suggestive statement, they wisely kept their mouths shut. "Now, if that's all, we've got a lot of work to do. Hop to it."

He helped Tyler haul in the rest of her tools from the truck before diving in to his own assignment. It was easy to lose himself in the symphony of power tools, the dance of teamwork. They demoed the remainder of the ceiling beneath the balcony to expose the joists and struts. Most were blessedly intact. Plans were adjusted slightly to accommodate additional replacement, then they began tying in new joists to the existing supports, framing out the rest of the balcony. It was heavy, brutal work, and Brody loved every minute of it. He'd forgotten exactly how much he loved the physicality of turning blueprints into reality with his own two hands.

He moved in and out of the lobby, over the course of the day. Each time he caught a glimpse of Tyler, she was bent over her machines, face fierce with concentration. The pile of moulding continued to grow at a steady pace. He didn't interrupt, not wanting to disrupt her progress, but the sight of her caused a pleasant little kick in his chest.

Paul ambled up and offered a bottle of water. "Bet you're gonna miss that on the next job.

Brody took the water and pretended not to understand him. "Miss what?"

Paul just arched an eyebrow and looked back toward Tyler. She shoved her safety goggles into her hair and stared critically at the match-up between two pieces of moulding. "Very easy on the eyes," he pronounced in his thick Brooklyn accent. "Damned talented, too. I'd even let her get her hands on my...tools."

"Watch it," Brody growled.

Paul just laughed. "What's the deal with you two? You a thing?"

Resigned that he couldn't avoid this conversation, Brody said, "We used to be."

As if sensing their eyes on her, Tyler turned. Catching his gaze, she smiled, really smiled, with the kind of unrestrained pleasure of their youth. The sight of it lit him up inside.

"Used to?" Paul muttered.

"It's complicated."

"Jensen, I get you're a detail man. You think of all the angles, all the ramifications, all the possible outcomes. That makes you damn good at the job. But if you're thinking about all that with her, then you're over-complicating shit."

"She's too important not to think about all that."

"Even more reason to keep it basic. You dig her. She digs you. Work with that."

Brody kept that in the back of his mind, through the rest of the work day. And when they wrapped, the full framework of new joists and struts installed, he headed to where Tyler was packing up her gear.

He picked up one of the pieces of moulding. "Looks good."

"It all needs proper sanding yet. I got the sanding blocks made, but it'll be tomorrow before I can finish that part." She tossed a tape measure into her tool box and rolled her shoulders.

"It's good work. A lot of work. And I say that means I owe you beer and a burger." *That's basic enough,* he thought.

Just a few weeks ago, she'd have hesitated, looking for some excuse or wrestling with what it might mean. Instead, she cocked her head and studied him, another of those smiles curving her mouth. "You taking anybody else out for beer and a burger?"

"Nope. Figured it'd be just me and my girl." He waited to see what her reaction to the possessive would be.

Her smile widened. "Good. I'd hate to have any third wheels on our date."

Progress, Brody decided, *is a beautiful thing.*

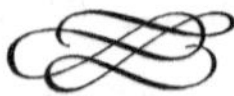

ZEKE HAMMEL WAS A thorough man. As the structural engineer charged with determining whether the theater was safe for public use, he needed to be. But Tyler fairly vibrated with impatience as he walked through to make his inspection. His very detailed, pain-staking inspection. She couldn't get a read on this guy. His weather-worn face made him look more like a stoic cowboy than an engineer. As he studied the new railing, Tyler half expected him to murmur, "Yup," and pop a plug of chewing tobacco into his mouth. She hung back a bit as Brody answered the questions, knowing she really had no place here but unable to stay away.

We did good work, she thought. *Miracle work.*

Brody had set out to make something that was merely functional, to get them through to the performance and beyond. But with the unexpected outpouring of help, they'd pulled off quite a bit above functional. It wasn't a full restoration—several rows of seats had been irreparably damaged—but they'd erased the destruction as wholly as they could. Brody had added additional columns into the design beneath the balcony, taking advantage of the missing seating to provide extra support to the structure. He was taking no chances on a repeat collapse.

Finished with the balcony, Zeke moved unhurriedly down the stairs to the lobby. Norah and her future mother-in-law, Mayor Sandra Crawford, followed. Brody paused to take Tyler's hand and give it a reassuring squeeze before they, too, headed downstairs.

The sun had still been up when they'd started. Tyler could see it was full dark beyond the lobby doors. The engineer was scribbling on a clipboard, flipping pages, checking things off. Norah and Sandra stood, arms linked. Tyler tightened her hold on Brody as Zeke signed something on one last page and looked up.

"Well?" Norah blurted.

In answer, Zeke handed over the clipboard.

She scanned the front page then let out a whoop, thrusting the clipboard into the air. "Pass!"

Relief gushed through Tyler, weakening her knees, even as she gave a bounce and a double fist pump, which had the effect of dragging Brody's arm up like a winning prize fighter. His hundred megawatt smile warmed her down to her toes.

"I'll have a more detailed report on your desk in a couple of days," Zeke continued, "but I figured given the time crunch you'd want approval as soon as possible."

"You figured right," Brody said.

Zeke crossed to him. "You do good work, Jensen. You ever decide to relocate back to Wishful, I'd like to work with you again."

Brody shook the offered hand. "Appreciate it."

With a brief word of farewell to the mayor and Norah, Zeke slipped out the doors, letting in a gust of cold evening air. As soon as he was out of sight, Brody let out a hoot and scooped Tyler up. "We did it!"

Tyler was laughing when his mouth took hers in a fervent, celebratory kiss. She felt the spark of it in her blood and kissed him enthusiastically in return, sliding her arms around his shoulders, her hands into his hair. By the time he set her on her feet again, she was breathless and dazzled.

"I pulled it off," he grinned. "Seemed only fitting to claim my reward."

"So you did," Tyler said. He'd pulled it off, preserved their history, and begun building something else while he was at it.

"If you're done locking lips for a bit," Norah said, eyes twinkling, "we need to get our butts to Speakeasy. Everyone is waiting to hear the news."

Brody saluted. "Yes, ma'am."

"Ride with me," Tyler said. "We'll get your truck later."

Once inside her truck, Brody collapsed into the passenger seat, head falling back against the rest. "God, what a crazy week. I can't remember when I slept less."

"Tired?"

"I should be, but no. I feel really buzzed. Hyped up on adrenaline."

"The crash will be brutal." She snaked out a hand, tangled her fingers with his across the console. It was a pleasure to give in to the desire to touch, to maintain physical contact.

"Yeah, but the party will be worth it." He lifted her hand to his lips, brushed them over her knuckles. "I really enjoyed working with you the last week. I've enjoyed pretty much everything about having you back in my life."

Tyler cut a glance at him in the flashing light of passing street lamps. He was relaxed as he watched her, his expression one of utter contentment. "We make a good team. Always did."

"Bookends," he murmured.

"Huh?"

"My mom used to call us bookends."

Tyler waited for the pang, but felt only a warm glow at the memory. "She'd be really proud of you, you know. You did a really good thing for the community this week, Brody."

"I did it for you." He said it simply, with no air of expectation. Just stating fact.

It was so...Brody. He'd always gravitated to grand gestures. Like mailing a plane ticket to Paris, for instance. He simply staggered her. He always had. As anxiety shifted to certainty inside her, Tyler decided it was time to make her own grand gesture.

She pulled out her phone, dialed Piper.

"Where are you?" she demanded. "Norah's here and we're all waiting!"

"We're going to be late," Tyler said. "Tell her not to wait."

"It something wrong?"

Tyler glanced over at Brody, who watched her intently. "No, everything is very definitely right." She ended the call, tossed the phone into the cup holder.

"Where are we going, Tyler?"

She reached for his hand again. "Home."

TYLER WAS ALREADY REACHING for him as she kicked open the door to her house. Brody had time only to say her name before she'd fused her mouth to his, and the well-intentioned speech he'd rehearsed on the rest of the drive over, about making certain she was sure about this, bled out of his mind. She was a fever in his arms, all desperate demand as she nipped and goaded, tugging at his clothes. His blood fired as he jerked her to him, molding that lean, muscled body to his as he plundered her mouth. Where she led, Brody followed, circling through what was probably a living room as they shed clothes, hands greedy for skin. With every inch of newly exposed flesh, he wanted more.

They bumped into the sofa. Brody bowed her over the back of it, lips burning a trail from her jaw, down her throat to the valley between lace-cupped breasts. Tyler's hand fisted in his hair as her hips ground against his. "More," she demanded.

Brody pulled her up, spun her in an erotic dance toward the hall. The taste of her was a drug, exquisite, addictive. As his hands fumbled with the clasp of her bra, she dragged her mouth from his and set her teeth to the juncture between his neck and shoulder.

Brody's control snapped. Pressing her back against the wall, he shoved down the lace and filled his hands with her breasts. Her low moan was a dark delight. Her hips moved in a restless, seeking rhythm against his as he took one budded nipple into his mouth and pleasured them both. He felt the tension coil through her, wanted to watch her ride that crest to the end. So he pressed a hand against her, firm and intimate, and watched her face as he slipped a finger into all that waiting heat. He kept watching, as he matched her instinctive rhythm and drove her relentlessly up. His name was a plea on her lips, as she shattered in his hands.

Brody hitched her up, wrapping those long legs around his waist. Her back to the wall, it would take only one thrust to sheath himself, to send them both spiraling into madness. But he wanted more from her than mindless pleasure. He wanted—*needed* more for them both. So he dropped his head to her shoulder and breathed in her scent, until he thought he could find some of that missing control, some semblance of finesse.

Tyler's hand moved across his shoulder, into his hair. "Brody?"

Her expression, when he lifted his head, was a strange mix of guarded vulnerability. Already preparing herself for rejection. God, he hated that was in her mind, hated that there was reason for it. Seeing her anxiety dulled the vicious edge of need, gave him the control he needed.

"Not here," he rasped. "Which way is the bedroom?"

Her face relaxed. "Last door on the left."

Brody could feel the gallop of her heart as he carried her the rest of the way down the hall. He'd had her desperate. Now he wanted her steeped in pleasure. In the bedroom, he let her slide down his body, then framed her face, as he had on stage weeks ago. It was confusion now, instead of the dread and anticipation, as he stroked her cheek. "I never thought I'd be here with you again." He brushed his lips over hers. "I don't want to rush through it. I want to make love with you, Tyler."

Her breath caught. "Brody."

"Shh." He dipped his head to her mouth, tasted her sigh as she melted against him. Her surrender was a gift he'd never expected, and he cherished it. Hands skimmed in long strokes meant to soothe, until her pulse turned slow and thick. He kept his pace easy, unhurried, sinking into the kiss layer by layer, easing her into a dance, though there was no music save what beat in his blood. No matter the time they'd lost, he wouldn't rush this.

The flavor of her seeped into him. He savored it as he took her deeper, splaying a hand over the warm skin of her back. The subtle play of muscle beneath his palm was fluid as water, as she swayed with him, her body, as always, responsive to every move of his. Tracing a hand up her spine, Brody pressed his lips to her fluttering pulse and eased her back on the bed.

He filled his hands with her, relearning the shapes and textures that had haunted his dreams. The subtle flare of hip. The strong arms. The column of that lovely throat. Tyler murmured his name, fingers threading in his hair, nails scraping lightly down his back. Her breath hitched and released as he savored, urging her slowly higher with lips and hands. Everything he asked, she gave without reservation, until at long last she whispered, "Please, Brody. Please."

He slipped inside her. Tyler arched up to take him, her eyes glazed with pleasure. And here was the homecoming he hadn't expected, hadn't even known he'd been yearning for, hadn't dared to even think about for years. Brody waited for her eyes to clear, to fasten on his before he began to move. The fingers he laced with hers were an anchor as they climbed. His pulse, his breath quickened as they circled higher, narrowing his focus, until all he could see, all he could feel, was her. Tyler wrapped her legs around his waist, holding him deep as she climaxed around him. Breathing her name, he let go and followed.

They lay tangled, skin damp and flushed from exertion. As soon as he had the muscle control to manage it, Brody rolled to the side, to keep from crushing her. He reached over to grab an edge of the comforter and rolled back, pulling her close. She snuggled into him, pressing her cheek to his chest and tangling their legs again. And for the first time since he'd left eight years ago, Brody felt completely at peace.

"Do you actually want to go to the party?" Tyler asked. "I mean, you're probably missing a rousing rendition of 'For He's a Jolly Good Fellow' with multi-part harmony."

"I think we have adequately proved that I do not require multi-part harmony to be roused."

She muffled a snort of laugher against his chest.

"Besides, that would involve actually moving from this spot, wouldn't it?"

"Yeah."

"Then no." He tightened his arm as she settled back against him and enjoyed the comfortable silence.

"Brody?" Tyler's voice was muffled.

He pressed a kiss to her hair. "Mmm?"

"Will you stay?"

He opened his eyes and stared at the wash of moonlight on the wall. Was she asking about tonight or for good? Either way he knew he couldn't make himself let her go.

Stroking a hand down her back, he pressed another kiss to her temple. "Yeah, I'll stay."

THE MAGIC IS BACK, Brody thought. It showed, in every movement, every perfectly delivered line as he and Tyler immersed themselves into their characters. The spark of it was contagious, spreading among the cast like wildfire, until even those less than stellar members of the chorus were upping their game, putting their absolute best foot forward. In the week since they'd gotten access to the stage again, the cast had been working extra hard to make up for the lost rehearsal time, and it was paying off.

Brody knew he was grinning like an idiot as Tyler and Piper danced their way toward him and Myles from stage left in their WAC uniforms. His grinning had been fairly constant, not diminished in the least by the good-natured ribbing offered up by their friends and some of the other cast members. Their absence at the post-inspection celebration hadn't gone unnoticed. But how could he care, when Tyler was his again? He slipped his arms around her, absorbing her flirtatious smile and feeling fireworks booming in his blood. Pouring some of that energy into the performance, he danced and twirled his way through the rest of "I Wish I Was Back In The Army" with as much panache as he could muster until, arm-in-arm with Tyler and Piper, he tapped his way off stage right.

A single, enthusiastic clap sounded from the back of the auditorium. Not Nate. Stepping back out onstage, Brody shaded his eyes from the lights but couldn't make out the newcomer as he approached.

"Well done," the man called. "This is exactly the kind of performance that would've made my father proud."

"Daniel." Nate slid into the aisle and strode to meet him. "I didn't expect to see you here. Decided to finally come by and take a gander at our efforts?"

The two men shook hands in greeting. The murmur of their voices wasn't loud enough to carry clearly to the stage.

"Who is this guy?" Brody muttered.

"Daniel Stanton," Tyler whispered. "Old Mr. Stanton's son. He left Wishful back when we were in high school, I think. Lives up in Oxford now."

So this was the stiff Norah sweet talked into letting them repair the theater. Brody studied him, taking in the lanky build, the receding hairline, and weak chin. His expression was affable enough, but something about the other man set off Brody's bullshit detector. The reaction was borne out when Nate burst out, "You're kidding me!" in a tone that suggested outrage rather than elation.

Daniel gave a *what-can-I-do* shrug and an apologetic smile Brody didn't buy for a minute.

Nate waved toward the stage with an expansive gesture that screamed sarcasm. "It's your news. You make the announcement."

Tyler slipped her hand into Brody's as Stanton headed for the stage. Brody could feel the tension thrumming through her, knew it was mirrored in the rest of their castmates, all of whom had spilled out from the wings to see what was going on.

"Y'all have put so much work into putting on this show," Daniel began. "I know my father would be incredibly touched by your efforts, most especially with the miracle you pulled off to repair the theater after the balcony collapsed. The end result is truly amazing."

"We're all waiting for the 'but', Mr. Stanton," Tyler said.

"But." He offered another of those apologetic smiles. "I'm afraid that *White Christmas* will be a farewell show instead of a fundraiser. The bank has decided to foreclose."

A cacophony of exclamations greeted this pronouncement.

"Can't you ask for a continuance? An extension? Something?" Tucker demanded.

"Done and done. We've been operating on an extension for the last several months. The bank has been bought out by another bank, and the new management is disinclined to allow that extension to continue. It was all I could do to get them to allow the show to finish. Come end of December, the Madrigal is closing its doors. I'm sorry."

Conversation exploded as everyone tried to comment at once. Brody heard Tyler's sound of disgust and distress and pulled her in for a hard hug. Stanton slipped out in the midst of the ensuing chaos.

Coward, Brody thought. *I'm surprised he had the guts deliver the news himself.*

"People. People! Settle down," Nate called. He waited for silence. "This is certainly disappointing news. It appears we've run out of time and options."

"So now what?" Myles asked.

Nate squared his shoulders. "Rehearsals will continue as planned. The show will open in three weeks. And it's going to be the best damned performance any of us has ever given. If we're going out, then by damn, we're going out with a bang."

There were remarks of half-hearted agreement with that, a few apathetic cheers, but it was hard for anyone to muster much enthusiasm.

Rehearsal wrapped after that. Tyler said nothing as she gathered her gear and walked out to Brody's truck. She remained silent on the drive back to her house, her arms curled around her bag like a teddy bear. As soon as he stopped, she slid out of the truck and trudged up the steps. There she stopped, swearing as she went purse diving for keys.

"Here, let me." He stepped past her to use the key she'd given him over the weekend.

Inside she tucked her bag into one of the clever little cubbies beside the front door as he dumped his keys into a decorative bowl.

Arms no longer full of bag, Tyler crossed them over her middle. "It's really over." Her words felt like heavy stones in the silence. "All that work, and for what? To see our history sold off and destroyed?" The bleak expression on her face tore at him.

Brody reached for her. "Tyler…"

She came into his arms, but her expression was mutinous. "Don't you dare tell me you can fix it. This isn't a broken pipe or some bad wiring. It isn't a cave-in or a restoration project anymore. This can't be fixed by any means you or I possess."

She wasn't wrong, so he didn't argue. And yet his mind spun, searching for a way—any way—because he couldn't bear to see her brutal disappointment.

"It was all for nothing," she pronounced, voice thick with tears she wouldn't let fall.

"It wasn't for nothing." Brody gave her a little shake. "It gave us *us* back. And that's worth more than anything else. The theater closing doesn't change that. It can't. We're more than our history, Tyler."

Her lips curved a little. "You've gotten smarter as you've gotten older."

"Just stating a fact." He curled his arms tighter around her as she burrowed in.

There was, he realized, so much more here for him than there had been, even at twenty-two. He wanted the time and the opportunity to explore it, to nurture it. Quite simply, he wanted the life he and Tyler always dreamed of. With the Babylon project quickly winding down, that was going to take an even bigger feat of mental acrobatics to sort than the financial problems of the Madrigal. Which meant that he had a lot more than punch-out work to discuss with Gerald, when he arrived later this week.

At the thought of his boss, Brody's mind sparked. The first niggle of an idea began to take shape.

Tyler tugged away. "I think I'm going to have a bath before bed."

"Sure."

As she started toward the back of the house, Brody began to turn over details, making mental lists of things to research, specifics that would have to be worked out.

"I wouldn't mind some company," she called.

"I never turn down such an invitation from a gorgeous woman." Brody headed back, deciding he wouldn't mention his idea to her. It was crazy. A long shot, at best. There was no reason to get her hopes up. But if he could come up with the right angle, the right pitch, there might be a way to save the theater.

"Can I get you anything else?" Tyler asked.

"Oh no, we're coming up on winter," Patty Spruill said. "The projects are slowing down at Casa Spruill. I just wanted to pick up the parts to fix that leaky shower faucet in the guest bath before all the kids come home for the holidays."

Tyler bagged up the O-ring cartridge replacement kit. "This will do it. And if you have any trouble, you give us a call. Or if you end up needing a plumber, I can recommend Ray Gentry or Leroy Dubois."

"Ha, that'll be the day," said Patty. "Sheldon Spruill does not call repairmen for things he can most certainly do himself. But thanks for the recs. If he breaks something, it'll be nice to have someone on reserve." Patty picked something up from in front of the register. "What's this?"

"Hm?" Tyler offered the bag and shifted to see what she had in her hand.

Patty held up a manila envelope. Frowning, Tyler took it and opened the clasp, shaking out the contents. A flight itinerary with confirmation numbers lay on top of the stack. She skimmed the details. Memphis to Dallas to Portland. Departure on January 3rd. Brody Jensen.

What are you up to? she wondered, laying the papers aside. "Brody must've left it behind at lunch. I'll get it to him later."

Patty smiled. "It's good to see you two back together."

"It's good to *be* back together," Tyler admitted.

"Well, we're all looking forward to your performance. I bought tickets for the whole family for opening night."

"Should be a good show. I think you'll enjoy it." Tyler tamped down the twinge that it would be the last opening night she'd ever have at the Madrigal.

Once Patty was out the door, she picked up the papers again and began to shuffle through them. She hadn't realized that she'd expected to see her name on an identical flight itinerary until she didn't find it. Instead, she found lists of addresses and contractors and a letter addressed to Brody on Peyton Consolidated letterhead. Tyler's eyes picked up isolated phrases.

...exemplary work...wrap up of Babylon project...exciting new opportunity...head up project from the beginning...expect you in Portland...

The papers fluttered down from Tyler's suddenly limp fingers. She barely heard the jingle of the bell over the roaring in her ears as two more customers entered the store.

Brody's leaving.

"Can you help us?"

She blinked at the young couple and struggled to pull her focus back. "Of course."

Her heart was pounding, her chest cranking tight like a vice around her lungs. Somehow she managed to get through the next fifteen minutes, giving advice on paint finish and paint colors before mixing two gallons of eggshell in a shade called Sierra Mist. As soon as they were gone, Tyler grabbed her keys and did something she absolutely never did. She closed the store in the middle of the afternoon and walked out.

Brody would be at the hotel job site this time of day. Her body was trying to shake, but she wouldn't let it. Ruthless, she fought back her growing panic and the tears that wanted to fall as the full impact of what she'd read began to sink in. This wasn't the time to jump to conclusions. There might be a perfectly reasonable explanation for the fact that he hadn't told her. Just because his boss wanted him to go to Portland for this job didn't mean he was going. Did it?

It gave us us back. They hadn't actually talked about this being more than a temporary thing, but when he kept saying things like that, didn't it mean something?

A sick, roiling sensation settled in Tyler's gut as she shoved through the plastic tarps hanging over the front of the building. The front desk had been installed, she noted. Furniture had been delivered to the bar area, still wrapped in plastic and foam. The swanky globes hung, glittering, over the long, glossy bar, and looked every bit as gorgeous as she'd imagined. Everywhere around her were signs of the project drawing to a close. Brody had said Gerald intended to do a soft launch for New Year's.

"You can't be in here!" A harried man Tyler didn't recognize rushed down the stairs. The clipboard under his arm and the wire rim glasses told her this had to be Gerald Peyton's assistant.

"You must be Louis. I'm Tyler Edison. We've spoken on the phone." There. Her voice was calm and even, without a glimmer of the fact she was falling apart on the inside. Still an actress after all. She offered her hand.

The man relaxed, giving her hand a perfunctory shake. "What

can I do for you, Ms. Edison? Is there a problem with any of our orders?"

"No, no. Everything's fine for the project. I'm looking for Brody Jensen."

"He's not here," Louis said. "He and Gerald are looking at some new commercial property down the street."

There was only one new commercial property down the street. The Madrigal. Tyler absorbed that blow, wondering that her legs didn't just give out on her.

"Do you want me to let him know you were looking for him when he gets back?"

"No, I think I'll just see if I can't catch up with him later."

Tyler wanted to run straight to the theater. But her feet felt like lead and her chest was clamping down even tighter, until she could hardly breathe. It couldn't be true. There had to be some other alternative to what she was imagining. She couldn't have gotten things with Brody so horribly wrong.

The Madrigal's lobby door was unlocked. Tyler slipped inside with no more than a whisper of footsteps on the worn red carpet. Hearing the murmur of voices in the auditorium, she edged to the door and tugged it open just wide enough to slip inside. The aisle lights were on dim and the stage was lit up as if for production. Brody and Gerald stood in front of the set for the Ed Harrison Show. The acoustics of the stage were such that she could hear their conversation all the way at the back where she stood in the shadows.

"—wanted to show the place to you without Sally, so we could actually talk about the possibilities without it getting all over town," Brody said.

"As always, I value your discretion. It's a unique and interesting space with lots of possibilities. The location is prime and would fit in perfectly with the rest of the conference facilities I want to put in up the block. Of course all the old stuff would need gutting and modernizing. The carpet and seats are worn out. We'd want to install a state-of-the-art projector system for presentations up here and update all this backstage space with all the nice behind-the-scenes amenities that help conferences run flawlessly. Unseen efficiency."

With every word, Tyler felt like vomiting.

"This was a marvelous idea," Gerald continued. "There simply wasn't the commercial space anywhere else in the downtown area, and with the zoning restrictions, we couldn't actually build anything to suit. This will enable us to expand the conference facilities to not only rival the Alluvian but outstrip them. And that means profits, my boy. You'll be long gone by that point, of course. As soon as things wind up here, I want you in Portland to deal with the retrofitting of the hotel I acquired last month. I sent you the specs already. The construction team is already in place, and their projections just aren't going to work for my schedule. I need your particular brand of management to get the ball rolling."

"Thanks, Gerald." Brody's voice sounded far away. "Your faith means a lot to me, and the hotel is an amazing opportunity—"

Tyler couldn't stay another minute. Fighting tears, she slipped silently back the way she'd come, walking away from the man who'd shattered all illusions that he'd be making a life with her.

THE FAINT HUM of the shower greeted Tyler as she stepped through the front door. She was grateful for the brief reprieve, for the chance to find her composure before facing Brody. Rehearsal had taken so much out of her with all that effort to try and appear normal when she was so raw. Piper hadn't bought it. Neither had her father. But she'd managed to put them both off, claiming exhaustion from juggling work and rehearsals. It wasn't a total lie.

Bringing Ollie to the bedroom as she usually did felt too much like fighting in front of the child, so instead, she settled him on his bed in the living room with a rawhide chew, before moving back to the bedroom to wait. The comparison was foolish and irrational. But she wasn't feeling particularly logical at the moment.

Brody emerged from the bathroom in a towel and a cloud of steam. "Hey, I can't find my stuff, have you seen—"

"It's here." Tyler picked up the duffel from the closet behind her and heaved it onto the bed.

He looked from the bag back to her.

Her heart pounded a vicious, relentless rhythm in her chest, until she felt like she would explode with the force of it. She needed cold, needed calm to get through this. Walking to the chair in the corner, she imagined a layer of ice coating her from head to toe, freezing out the hot burn of pain that had been lodged beneath her breastbone since she'd opened that envelope.

Brody remained standing in the bathroom doorway, dripping onto the carpet as he held the towel loosely around his hips. His expression hadn't settled into anything yet—still somewhere between *I don't understand what's going on* and *everything is clearly not okay.*

"You're dripping," Tyler said.

He moved to the bag, peered inside. "You packed."

"I did."

"Are we going somewhere?"

"No."

Saying nothing, Brody pulled out clothes. When he dropped the towel to put them on, she looked away, then glanced back under her lashes. She hated that she had to look. But this was the last time she was going to see him outside of rehearsal, and she needed to memorize the lean, muscular lines of his body.

He shrugged into a shirt. "Tell me."

Tyler had spent the afternoon working out this speech, struggling to find the best way to present this so as not to start a fight. She couldn't handle a fight. She was too close to breaking.

"I thought I could do this," she said quietly. "I thought I could pick back up where we left off. But we aren't twenty-one anymore. We're different people than we were when you left. Different people, who want different things, who are in two different places in their lives."

"What are you saying?"

"It's done. I'm done." The words came out with more of an edge than she intended, but it fit with the coolheaded calm she was trying to project.

Brody flinched, his eyes narrowing at the tone. "You want me to move out."

He'd barely moved in. But then, he hadn't *really* moved in. He'd been living out of a bag, like the guest that neither of them acknowledged he was.

How nicely that fit with her new understanding of him.

"I think that would be best." God, it hurt her to say it, but rationally, what other choice was there? It didn't matter that him leaving was the worst possible thing, that it was exactly what she didn't want. She had to be the one to end this. It had to be on her terms. She couldn't just wait for him to destroy her again, not in front of the whole damned town, where she'd be the object of everyone's well-intended compassion. Again. Of the two of them, she was staying. She was the one who had to live with this.

"What if I don't?"

A spark of hope lit in her chest. *Then fight for us, Brody. Fight for me.* Tyler couldn't speak, too afraid that if she did, all she'd manage would be pleas for him to stay. She wouldn't beg. The scraps of her pride were the only thing she had left.

"I guess you've already made up your mind," he said.

It would be so goddamned easy to bend and give him an in, to let him convince her to allow this to play out a few more weeks. But she couldn't do that. Couldn't bear it.

"This was temporary," she began. "I knew that when I decided to get involved with you again." A lie. "My life is here, in Wishful. Yours is out there in the wide world. I tried to ignore that, tried to pretend that eight years of becoming different people didn't happen. But it did, and I'm not interested in pretending anymore. Playtime's over."

"You think I've been playing with you?" Now it was his voice with the edge.

Tell me. Tell me you haven't. Tell me this is real. Tell me you aren't walking away.

The sound of the zipper closing made Tyler flinch. Brody picked up his bag, slung it over his shoulder in a manner that suggested he'd rather be hurling it at the nearest wall. His eyes were narrowed, his lips compressed. "Good to know. I'll see you at rehearsal, Tyler."

She listened to his retreating footsteps, feeling her heart sink with each step. At the sound of the door closing, she shot to her feet and stumbled down the hall toward the front door. There, she stopped herself, wrapping both arms around her middle to ward off the shaking as she stared at the wood panels, willing it to open again. But, of course, it didn't. Every cell in her body strained toward the door, urging her to run after him, whether he thought her a fool or not. But she didn't move. And when she heard the engine of his truck turn over, heard the sound of him pulling out of the drive, she fell to her knees and wept.

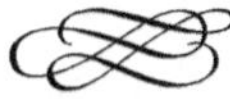

THE BABYLON JOB WAS all but done.

There were lists of final details to be tended to—always some kind of last minute, unexpected thing. But by and large, the construction was complete. The interior design crew was kitting out the rooms upstairs with the furniture that had been delivered earlier in the week. Cam, as landscape architect, was overseeing the planting of the hanging gardens on the roof. As Brody sat alone at the gleaming mahogany bar, he knew he should already be moving on. The portion of the job under his purview was done. Because of his commitment to the show, Gerald was leaving him to take care of the details that Louis normally handled. But even that should be handed off to the new manager in a few weeks. He'd done a hell of a job, beating even his best record for the company in terms of bringing in the project ahead of schedule.

None of it meant a damn thing.

Brody felt none of the usual pleasure in a job well done, no joy over the finished product. Because it all meant he was that much closer to being out the door and on to the next job. And for the first time in eight years, that was no longer enough.

Cracking open a bottle of bourbon from the newly stocked bar, Brody poured himself a glass and avoided looking at the envelope full of details on the Portland job that Louis had sent over that afternoon. Brody had lost the first one.

"You been holding out on us, boy-o!"

Brody looked over his shoulder to see Tucker clomping his way across the room, Cam on his heels.

"Neither of you is supposed to be here," Brody said.

"We are on a mission," Tucker announced. "And since it's all of benefit to you, you can pour us some of whatever it is you're drinking there."

Brody didn't relish company for his brood, but he knew his friends weren't going to leave him be until they'd said whatever they had to say. With a marked lack of enthusiasm, he circled around to the other side of the bar and grabbed a couple more glasses.

"Much obliged." Tucker accepted the glass, took a testing sip. "Mmm. Smooth."

Cam took his own glass and used it to point at Brody. "Now, it has become increasingly clear over the last week that you have a bug up your butt about something and, given that Tucker and I have actually *seen* you on multiple occasions when you have heretofore been joined to the hip with the lovely Miss Edison, we conclude that all is not well in paradise."

He and Tucker exchanged a look. "What did you do?" they demanded in unison.

Brody glared at them. "Not a goddamned thing. And if you're both going to be assholes instead of friends, I'm not sharing."

Tucker moved his low ball out of Brody's reach. "Let's try this again. What happened?"

"Hell if I know. She came home from rehearsal last week and asked me to move out. Already had my bag packed."

"Did you have a fight? Because groveling is always advisable in that case," Cam said.

"She wasn't angry." If she'd been angry, he would've had something to fight against. But that calm, cool finality gave him no leverage. "She just said she couldn't do it anymore—that we'd both known it was temporary from the start, and she didn't see the point in pretending anymore." God that burned. When had he ever given the impression that his intentions were temporary?

"Is that what you were doing?" Tucker demanded. "Because I'm not too gimpy to kick your ass."

The slap of the glass as Brody slammed it down on the table echoed off the high ceiling. "I love her."

"Simmer down," Cam ordered. "It's a fair question. If Tyler said it, then clearly you did or did not do something to spark that thought. So what was it?"

"Why is this on me? It was her decision."

"Do you want help figuring out what went wrong or not?" Tucker asked.

"She's made up her mind," Brody said. That had been painfully obvious in the set expression on her face, in the fact that she wouldn't meet his eyes.

"And you're clearly totally okay with that," Cam said, "what with the Little Mary Sunshine attitude you've been sporting all week."

Brody gritted his teeth. "Of course I'm not."

"She said it was temporary, so she went into it expecting you to leave," Tucker said. "Did you?"

"I don't know. I didn't think beyond having her back in my life. Having her back was like a miracle. And by the time I realized I was going to have to figure out how to make it work, she's kicking me out."

"This might have something to do with it." Cam tapped the envelope he'd opened and pointed at the flight itinerary on top. "You're leaving for Portland in January. If she heard about that, could be she's just cutting things off now to make sure it ended on her terms."

"For fuck's sake, *I'm* practically just hearing about it. Where would she have heard?" Brody stopped, cutting himself off. He *had* lost the first packet of information. If she'd found it… He shook his head. "None of it was even finalized until after she kicked me out. And why wouldn't she *talk* to me about it?"

"Because you have a history of leaving without a word," Tucker said. When Brody would've spouted off again, he held up a hand. "It doesn't matter the whys of what happened before. You weren't here to see what that did to her. We were. We were the ones who picked up the pieces. It was bad, Brody. Really damned bad. There's not a one of us who would blame her for not wanting to go through that again."

Jesus, would he ever be free of the guilt from that? "I'd never do that to her. Not deliberately."

"Did you tell her that?" Cam asked. "Did you tell her, at any point, explicitly, 'Look, Tyler, this temporary thing is not going to work for me. I have no idea how we're going to make it work, but I love you and I want more?'"

"Do actions count for *nothing?*"

Tucker looked at Cam. "No," they said.

"Women need the words," Cam said. "Which means we have to man up and say them, no matter how obvious all of it seems to us."

"Sometimes we need the words too. She's never asked me to stay." Not once since that unguarded moment after they'd become lovers again.

"Then you're not only stupid, you're blind," Tucker pronounced. "Just because she hasn't spelled it out doesn't mean she doesn't want you to. She'd never have let you back into her life otherwise. Tyler's not the type to give an ultimatum. She *can't* leave, can't change the responsibilities she has here, so the change has to be on you. She'd never outright ask you to give up things for her. She'd feel too much like she was guilting you into it."

What, exactly, did she think he'd be giving up? "How is saying what you want a guilt trip?"

Cam shrugged. "I don't know. Seems to me you both suck at saying what you want. I speak from personal experience when I say you should go grovel and work on that."

Brody thought of that carefully blank face, the hint of banked temper in her eyes. What was behind her mask? "I'm not sure she's in a place where she's interested in listening to anything."

"Then I guess you'll just have to do it in a way she can't ignore."

How could a house where she'd lived alone for the last five years feel so empty after having a guest for only a week?

Because you never saw Brody as a guest. Tyler clutched a pillow to her chest and stared up at the living room ceiling. *Because you built this place for him, for both of you, and part of you has just been waiting all these years for him to come home.*

Well, that wasn't happening again. The pain of that was quick and deep and familiar. For the last week, fresh stabs had struck her everywhere she turned in the house. And that didn't even begin to cover the misery of rehearsal. There they danced, and Brody's touch was light and impersonal. That in itself felt like a slap. Dancing had always been an intimacy, a shared pleasure. And now...

Well what the hell did you expect? You took him back, and you kicked him to the curb. Now you have to deal with the consequences.

Still, Tyler couldn't see getting involved with Brody again as a mistake. She'd wanted closure. In truth, she'd wanted a hell of a lot more than that. But closure was what she'd gotten. No more wondering why he never came back for her or if he ever would. After the play was over, he wouldn't be coming back to Wishful, back to her. It was done now, settled with the kind of finality their previous parting had lacked. The part of her that had spent all these years waiting could finally move on.

Whatever the hell that looked like.

Moving on was somewhere well on the other side of a pain she'd done her best to forget.

Part of the process, she thought. *Been there, done that. Burned the t-shirt.*

Ollie barked, thumping his tail.

"Potty?" she asked.

He barked again.

"At least you're simple." Tyler rolled off the sofa. "Food. Water. Potty. Cuddles. We've got all that covered, buddy boy." She pulled open the door, scooped Ollie up and headed outside.

"Gotcha."

Tyler closed her eyes at the triumphant tone in Piper's voice from where she'd been hiding out of sight on the other side of the grill. *I should've known that a text announcing I had a highly contagious stomach bug wouldn't keep her away.*

"We've been worried about you." Norah unfolded from the chaise lounge.

Crap.

Ignoring them both, she continued on into the yard, setting Ollie down so he could do his business.

"You know, I was pretty sure you were lying about being sick," Piper said. "But you look awful."

"Thanks. You've seen for yourself that I'm not well. Now you can go report back to whoever you're reporting back to and let me go back to bed." Where she'd been spending all of her time when she wasn't at the store or at rehearsal, trying to pretend that everything was fine when, in fact, she was exhausted and heartsick.

"Do you know me *at all?*" Piper asked.

"Unfortunately, yes. Didn't anybody ever teach you to respect a brood?"

"We brought pizza, Ben and Jerry's, and chicken noodle soup," Norah announced before heading in through the back door and making for the kitchen.

That was it then. There'd be no ejecting them now. At least they'd come bearing food. Dinner the last two nights had been a bowl of dry Peanut Butter Crunch cereal, the last shred of Brody in the house.

Piper waited until she got Ollie settled on his living room bed to speak again. "I'm going to use my super duper powers of observation here and hazard a guess that Brody is no longer staying with you."

Staying, Tyler thought with a pang. *Even she knew it was really temporary.*

"No."

Piper crossed to the stereo, turned it on. After two bars of The Cure rolled out of the speakers, she stabbed it off again. "Oh honey, it's worse than I thought. Lay it out. Tell us what he did in order that we may conceive of the appropriate punishment for him."

God love Piper for immediately thinking it was all his fault.

"Nothing."

"You don't want to punish him? Norah, quick, bring the Ben and Jerry's. This is serious."

"He didn't do anything." That was the problem. "I asked him to move out."

"You—" Piper cut herself off. "I think I need the Ben and Jerry's too."

Norah came back with the ice cream and three spoons. "Why did you ask him to move out?"

"Because I needed him to go on my terms. I needed to keep something when he walked away, even if it was only my pride." Not that the shriveled husk of that was much comfort under the circumstances.

Piper immediately sank to the sofa and put an arm around Tyler's shoulders. "Why now?"

"Because I couldn't keep up the charade anymore. He's not staying. He was never staying."

"Okay, I know that was the case when he got here," Norah said, "but that really isn't the impression I've had since you got back together. What makes you so sure he hasn't changed his mind?"

"Because I found the flight itinerary and all the details of his next job. He's leaving for Portland come January, and he didn't tell me."

"Oh honey." Norah set down the ice cream and wrapped her arms around Tyler from the other side.

Sandwiched between her friends, Tyler felt tears begin to burn. Fighting them back, she choked out, "It gets worse. He's talked his boss into buying the Madrigal to turn into some kind of awful conference center. After everything we did to save it, all that talk about preserving our history, now he's leading the charge to destroy it."

"He what?" Piper demanded, a dangerous glint in her eye. "He told you he was doing that?"

Tyler shook her head. "I went to find him after I found the stuff about Portland. He was there, at the theater, going over the whole thing with Gerald Peyton. I heard all of it. They never knew I was there."

"Did you ask him about it? About any of it?" Norah asked.

"What was the point? I heard with my own ears, saw it written in black and white. And when I asked him to go, he just *went*. No fuss, no fight, no argument. Who *does* that?"

Norah was wearing her very careful negotiation face. "Well, honey, what did you expect him to do?"

"If it really mattered, if *I* really mattered, he would've stayed and at least hashed out what was wrong."

"Why didn't you tell him what was wrong?" Piper asked. At Tyler's glare, she held up a hand for peace. "He's a man, ergo he's dense. You can't expect him to be a mind reader. You jumped right on to the end of the fight without giving him a chance at participating and defending himself."

"Did you ever ask him to stay?" Norah asked.

She thought of the night they'd become lovers again, of the question that had slipped out in that unguarded moment. He'd thought she was asking him to stay for the night, not forever. And she hadn't felt the need to say it again, not when they had seemed to be so clearly on the same track. She never dreamed she'd been so wrong.

A niggle of doubt wormed its way into her mind. If she'd asked him—explicitly, outright asked him to stay—would it have made a difference?

"How can I do that?" she whispered.

"It's very simple." Piper put her hands on Tyler's face like the genie in *Aladdin*. "You say, 'Brody, I love you. I want you to stay.'"

Tyler shoved her hands away. "Right. And risk that he says no. Or worse, that he stays and grows to resent me because of it? I can't bear that."

"You don't know he'd do either of those things," Norah pointed out.

"I don't know that he won't. The only way I'll truly know is if he comes to me himself, of his own volition."

It struck her then. The truth of her situation. It *had* all been a mistake. Because after all these years, she was still waiting for him. She didn't get closure. All she'd done was reopen an old wound she used to know how to live with.

1 WEEK 'TIL SHOW

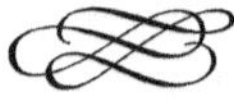

THIS WAS IT. THE last dress rehearsal they'd ever have in the Madrigal. As she stood in the dressing room, surrounded by the scatter of makeup, hair products, and all the other flotsam and jetsam of costuming, Tyler wanted to weep. It was simply too much to bear. Once this show was over, she'd have nothing left to hang on to. Brody would be gone, and the theater would be destroyed. And every day she passed it, she would have a flagrant reminder that he hadn't been the man she believed him to be.

"Hurry up!" Piper hissed from the door. "We're almost on!"

Tyler hurried through the rest of her costume change and took her position, real feather fan in hand. The smile she forced for the number felt like it would shatter her face, but her voice, her choreography was on point. At least now everyone would believe her lack of spark was due to the foreclosure rather than Brody. Except for Brody, at least.

He watched her, dark eyes far more serious than the role dictated. If it had still been temper in his gaze, he'd have been easier to ignore, but it was concern she saw as she traded lines and plotted matchmaking with him on stage. Tyler forced herself not to get lost or forget her lines. She thought she managed well enough, as Nate didn't stop the rehearsal for redirection. But Brody caught her in the wings between scenes.

"Hey, you okay?" he asked.

"Fine." Tyler knew the smile she shot him was more of a wince.

Brody lowered his voice. "You forget, I actually know you."

"I used to think I knew you." She moved away from him for the next costume change.

"What's that supposed to mean?" he demanded.

"We don't have time for this, Brody. I have to get changed."

Brody cursed, and Tyler felt the sizzle of his temper as he let her walk away. It lit a fire under her own, while she slipped into the next dress. How could he not know, not understand what he'd done? She was still simmering when she met him on stage again, and they sparked off each other as they performed.

Hardly the magic everyone expects, she thought as the curtain dropped for a set change.

"Cut!" Nate called.

Now they'd done it. They'd screwed things up with their personal crap badly enough that he'd stopped a dress rehearsal.

The curtain lifted again, and Tyler braced herself for a lecture. But Nate wasn't paying attention to them. Instead he was talking to someone in the aisle. Two someones. Squinting, she tried to make out who it was. Norah? What was she doing here?

"Raise the house lights, please," Nate shouted.

As the auditorium lights came up, Tyler felt her blood run cold as she recognized Brody's boss in his impeccable suit.

Norah and Gerald walked to the front of the auditorium, beside the orchestra pit. "Sorry for the interruption, y'all," Norah said, "but I knew you'd want to be the first to know. As you're aware, the Madrigal went into foreclosure with the bank a couple of weeks ago. The old girl isn't in the greatest of shape, and our various fund raising efforts weren't enough to keep the wolf from the door. But I am happy to report that the theater is off the market. The sales paperwork has been filed with the bank."

A low murmur of surprise swept through the cast.

Norah continued, "I'd like to introduce you to the new owner of the Madrigal Theater, Gerald Peyton. He wanted to come talk to all of you and tell you a bit about what he has planned."

Gerald stepped up, thanked Norah for her introduction.

Tyler's shoulders went rigid and she closed her eyes, waiting for the blow.

"I'm not from here," Gerald began, "but through my business dealings in the community, I've come to develop a true fondness for Wishful and its unique history. When I first heard of the availability of this property, my initial thought was to incorporate it into the same complex I'm developing up the street. But one of your own has worked very hard to convince me that there are other more…suitable alternatives that will maintain the integrity and history of the theater, while continuing the theme of urban redevelopment in downtown Wishful."

Tyler's head shot up and her heart began to pound.

"Brody, perhaps you'd like to tell them the rest," Gerald suggested. "It is your idea, after all."

Brody stepped forward to address the assembled cast, crew, and orchestra. "Y'all might've noticed I've looked half dead the last week during rehearsals. I apologize for that. I've been getting very little sleep, while I put together a proposal for Gerald about the Madrigal and her potential. For the record, I don't recommend anybody use AutoCAD while high on Mountain Dew." A chuckle swept through his audience.

"Gerald's new non-profit organization will be submitting a grant in the next month that's geared toward the first in a multi-phase project to create a state-of-the-art performing arts center. First and foremost, we're going to restore the theater. She's going to get outfitted with the latest in lighting and sound technology, while receiving a makeover to the lobby and auditorium that will return it to its original splendor."

A whoop went up from the crowd. Tyler felt her knees go weak. Brody grinned and held up his hands for quiet. "That's only the first stage. Ultimately we want to expand to include a concert hall and an additional outdoor performance space beyond the central park lands, for outdoor concerts and theater productions. Those projects will depend upon the securing of additional grant funding and revenues generated by continued and expanded performances of the complex. If you're interested in seeing what the proposed venues look like, I've been working on the plans for the last couple of weeks. But the important take home here is that The Madrigal is safe."

The Madrigal is safe. The words echoed through Tyler's brain. Brody met her gaze across the stage, cocking his head in question at her no doubt stunned expression.

Oh God. I had it all wrong.

Congratulations were tossed like confetti, and the generally dismal mood that had haunted rehearsals since they announced the foreclosure finally dissipated. Half the cast launched into a rousing rendition of "For He's a Jolly Good Fellow," while others burst into spontaneous jigs. Nate let it go on for a good five minutes, before calling everyone back to order and getting the dress rehearsal back on track.

Gerald came up to the edge of the stage and shook Brody's hand. "Good luck with the show. I'm afraid I won't be here during the run. I'm flying out tomorrow morning. But I'll see you on the third."

Tyler felt like the top had blown off her head. It was a minor miracle that she remembered her lines and choreography through the rest of the performance. The numbness started to wear off about the time they finished resetting the stage for opening night. She raced through changing back to street clothes. Piper strode in as she was hopping toward the dressing room door, pulling on her shoes.

"Tyler, did you—"

"I have to talk to Brody," she interrupted.

"I think he already left."

"Shit." Tyler pushed passed her, racing out to the parking lot.

He was tugging open the door of his truck when she burst outside.

"Brody!"

He tossed his bag into the front seat before turning to face her, bracing his arms on the open door and the frame of the cab.

Tyler slowed, trying to get a handle on her thoughts as she approached him. Now that he was staring at her, expectation on his face, she didn't know what she was going to say, only that she couldn't leave things as they had been.

"It's a really lovely thing you're doing for the theater," she began carefully. "Why didn't you tell me you were working on this?"

Brody shrugged. "It was a long shot. I didn't want to get your hopes up—or anybody else's—in case Gerald didn't go for it. I saw you when the announcement was made. You were surprised by the news. Why?"

She rocked back on her heels and dropped her gaze. "Because I heard you when you brought Gerald to see the theater. I was in the back of the auditorium. I heard his plans for the conference center and how he wanted to change everything. And I thought you'd encouraged him."

Anger and insult warred on his face as he stepped toward her. "Is *that* what all this was about? You thought I was helping destroy the theater?"

Tyler refused to allow herself to bend beneath the shame. "Part of it," she admitted. "I misjudged you, and I—I wanted to apologize for that."

"Then you still mean what you said."

Tyler wavered.

You don't have to hurt. Not yet. The tiny, sly voice poked at her. *He didn't want this. He'd take you back if you just relented.*

It was tempting—so tempting—the thought of having these last weeks with him and taking whatever time they had left. But how could she do that to herself? For all that she'd truly meant her attempt at living a *carpe diem* life where Brody was concerned, she didn't truly believe it was worth the extra pain. What progress she'd made since she'd ended things was incredibly hard won. Sliding back into any kind of temporary arrangement with him would do far more harm than good.

No, better to stay the course and be strong. She just had to survive the next three weeks. Then she'd finally get that clean break and her chance to start over.

"Yes." She trembled as she said it.

Brody's face softened. Stepping into her space, he cupped her cheek, sliding his fingers into her hair. "I miss you."

She swallowed the knot of tears in her throat. "I miss you, too."

Tyler half expected him to press her back against the truck, to take her mouth in one of those scorching, claiming kisses. Part of her wished he would. But Brody held still, and she realized he was waiting for her to close the distance between them. The distance she'd put there.

It would be a mistake.

Tyler stepped back. "Good luck in Portland, Brody. I wish you all the best."

The warmth of his fingers lingered against her skin as she walked away.

~

Good luck in Portland.

She knew. She knew he was leaving for Portland, and she'd said nothing. No demands for answers, no indication she wanted him to stay. Except for the bald pain on her face as she wished him all the best.

Why was she doing this? How could she possibly have believed he'd willingly destroy the theater?

Brody started to go after her, to push for the fight she avoided, so they could get everything out into the open. But tomorrow was opening night, and she was having enough trouble keeping to her role as it was. Blowing things wide open would likely just leave more wounds between them, and there was no way they could pull an understudy substitution this late in the game. He didn't *want* an understudy substitution. He wanted Tyler. So he curled his hands around the door frame and watched her walk away.

Shortly after leaving the theater, Brody found himself pulling into a space in front of Dinner Belles. This late the diner was empty but for a couple of open textbooks on one empty table. He didn't know what he was doing here except that he was too restless to go home and a slice of pie made thinking more palatable. He slid into a booth and flipped open his organizer. It was full of details on the Portland job, contacts, schedules, supply lists, projections and estimates. All the things that were part and parcel of his trade, the things that had dragged him up the ladder at Peyton Consolidated and landed him this opportunity. It was what he'd been working for all these years.

There was no thrill to his success of being appointed to manage the project from the get-go. He studied the various elevations of the new building design, and all he saw were details. Meaningless, empty details.

"What can I get you, Brody?"

He tensed as he looked up to find Corinne standing beside the table, a coffee pot in one hand. But there was no evidence of the flirtatious smile she usually aimed his way.

"Coffee," he said. "And a slice of whatever pie's left."

"There's a piece of lemon meringue with your name on it." She leaned in, efficiently flipped over the mug at his elbow and filled it without spilling a drop. And she did it all without stepping into his personal space. "I'll be right back with that pie."

Curious, Brody watched her as she crossed to the rack on the counter and plated up his slice. She looked different, somehow. He thought maybe she'd put on a few much-needed pounds since he'd first come back.

"You changed your hair," he said, as Corinne set the pie in front of him.

Self-conscious, she lifted a hand to her all dark locks, pulled back in a low pony tail. "Seemed like time for a change," she said.

It made her blue eyes stand out more and softened her face. "Looks nice," he said.

Her cheeks pinked at the compliment. Brody didn't think he'd ever once seen Corinne Dawson embarrassed.

"Thanks. Um, can I get you anything else?"

Without the automatic defensive barrier against her flirtation, Brody noted the dark circles under her eyes, the tired set to her shoulders. It was easier to see her as a person, as a single mom who'd got the short end of the stick in life rather than the girl he'd gone to high school with. He found himself saying, "Why don't you have a cup of coffee with me? I don't figure anybody else'll be coming in before closing."

Corinne glanced over at the open textbooks. "I should really—"

"Study?" he asked.

She nodded.

"Five minutes," he said. "The break will do you good."

After another moment of indecision, she retrieved her own coffee cup from the table and slid in across from him.

"What are you studying?" he asked.

"Nursing. I'm just taking a couple of classes this semester. Mama Pearl doesn't mind if I do homework when things are slow."

Brody smiled. "She takes good care of folks."

"She's been wonderful to me and Kurt. She's the one that encouraged me to go back to school. Lance never—" She cut herself off and took a quick sip of coffee.

"Lance is your ex?"

Corinne gave a short, jerky nod.

Sensitive subject here, he thought. "Sounds like you're well rid of him."

"You have no idea," she muttered. Squaring her shoulders, she mustered a smile. "So, opening night is tomorrow. I'm surprised Tyler's not in here with you. Isn't that a post-dress rehearsal tradition or something?"

It was Brody's turn to hide his expression in his coffee cup. "We aren't...together."

"For God's sake, why not?" The utter shock in her voice had him looking up.

"I think," he said slowly, "that I screwed it up somehow. Again."

Corinne thunked her mug on the table. "Then you need to figure out how to fix it."

Brody lifted a brow. "That is...not the reaction I expected from you."

She waved a hand dismissively. "Flirting with you was a compulsion from the old days. I've got plenty on my own plate without adding a man into the equation. And anybody with eyes in their head can see that you and Tyler belong together. You always did."

He sifted through the vague sense of insult and surprise. "Then why did you always try so hard?"

Corinne's cheeks colored again, deeper this time. "Because she had what I wanted. It wasn't you so much as someone like you. No one has ever looked at me the way you look at her. Like the sun rises and sets in her eyes. You respect her and you understand her. The pair of you were always so perfectly matched, like...I don't know—"

"Bookends," Brody murmured.

"Yeah," she agreed. "I was jealous of that, and I didn't know how to find that for myself. I still don't, but I've got other priorities now. Like raising my son to be a better man than his father. The point is, if something is wrong between you and Tyler, you have to fix it. You can't let the gift of that kind of relationship go just because stuff got hard."

"I wasn't the one who let go," he said.

"Apparently you weren't the one who fought to hold on either," Corinne said. "I don't know what you two fought about, and it doesn't matter. She's in love with you. She always has been, always will be. And if you walk away from that, you're exactly the idiot I thought you were eight years ago." She slid out of the booth and pulled the ticket from her apron pocket. "It'll be $3.25 for the pie and coffee. The advice is free." She laid it on the table and strode back into the kitchen.

Brody sat in stunned silence for several long minutes. Laying a twenty-dollar bill beside his uneaten pie, he walked out. He opened his truck, tossed in the organizer, then shut the door again. His mind too full to drive, he began to walk the quiet streets of downtown Wishful. Corinne's remarks bounced around like a pinball, adding to the weight of what Cam and Tucker had said.

He knew now what was at the root of Tyler breaking things off. Despite his lingering insult over the fact that she could've believed he'd truly have allowed the theater to be destroyed, when they'd put so much into preserving it, he understood her self-protective actions. For all that what had happened eight years ago was a terrible mistake, she had years of pain believing it had been deliberate. That wasn't so easily overcome by logic, especially not if circumstances had led her to believe he was going to do it again.

The question was, how was he going to fix it? Cam had said she'd need the words. But which words, and how? Brody didn't want to offer her the uncertainty of not knowing how things could work. He felt like he owed her more than that. He needed to work out the details.

Stopping in front of the Babylon, he looked up at the classic Georgian facade. He was damned good at details.

A breeze gusted through the trees, snaking under his collar. Brody shivered. Damn, it had finally gotten cold. He really ought to get back to the truck. But instead of turning back, he found himself drawn into the dark of the green, toward the fountain that was the heart of Wishful. Moonlight gleamed off the faint ripples on the surface. He bent and trailed his fingers through the frigid water. Once upon a time, he'd tossed in his coin, made his wish, and been disappointed. But maybe he'd been doomed to disappointment because he'd had no faith. Hope and faith were inextricably intertwined. You couldn't really have one without the other. Getting Tyler back was going to take a massive leap of faith.

As he stood beside the water, Brody felt the first stirrings of a plan begin to take form. Digging in his pocket, he pulled out a quarter, rolling it habitually across his knuckles, holding his wish clear in his mind before tossing the coin in with a splash.

"Hope springs eternal," he muttered.

OPENING NIGHT

TYLER STARED AT THE vase of bright yellow tulips on the dressing table. She didn't need to see the card to know they were from Brody. It was another of those show traditions.

"Aren't you going to read the card?" Piper asked.

She was almost afraid to open it. Her resolve was so weak at this point, she didn't know if she could hold up against him if he decided to press the issue. But the card only read, *Break a leg, beautiful* in his familiar, blocky handwriting. "Just the usual," Tyler said.

"Did you talk to him last night?"

"Yes." And yet there'd been so much unsaid. But it didn't matter now. He'd made his choice, and she'd made hers. They had a show to perform.

Tyler could see the struggle on Piper's face, desperate to ask more. But she'd wait because now wasn't the time. *And thank God for it.*

"Ten minutes to curtain!" The call swept through backstage like wildfire, sending them all into flurries of motion.

Tyler did her best to put Brody out of her mind, to finish her makeup and slip into the bathrobe that was her first costume for the night. She was in the wings when the opening overture began, watching as the curtain lifted on the Italian theater of World War II and Brody and Myles entertaining the troops. This was it. The last opening night show she'd ever have with Brody. A part of her ached even as she enjoyed his performance. Then it was time for her own, and she had no more opportunity to think.

As the show got rolling, Tyler managed to immerse herself in the role. She owed it to her castmates, to the Madrigal, to give it her all. But her all still wasn't feeling right. Not until Piper ad-libbed a slap to her butt with a feather fan and startled a laugh out of her. This was supposed to be *fun.* An outlet for joy. It was time to remember that it wasn't all about Brody. Loosening up, Tyler slid properly into the guise of Judy Haynes. She preened and flirted, shamelessly getting caught at playing the angle to get Wallace and Davis to come check out their sister act. So she was smiling when she rose from the table and accompanied Phil to the dance floor.

Tyler knew the moment Brody touched her for their first number that something had changed. For all that they couldn't seem to communicate in words, they'd always been able to speak through dance. The hand he curled around her waist was warm, firm, and proprietary, not the impersonal hold he'd been using recently. Part of her thrilled to the sensation and wanted to arch into his touch. It was instinct to flow into the rhythm of their movements and follow his lead. By the time her brain kicked in to question that instinct, the dance was over and they were transitioning to the next scene.

The pressure of continuing to go through the motions and remembering lines kept Tyler from dwelling on anything more personal for too long. So when they reached the engagement party kiss, she didn't feel the expected dread as Brody lowered his mouth to hers.

I miss you.

She felt the echo of his words in the lingering warmth of his mouth against hers, in the brush of his fingers over her cheek before he turned away to continue the scene. It wasn't the deliberate erosion of defenses he'd pulled the first time, but his kiss stirred her nonetheless, slipping behind the pitiful walls she'd managed to erect around her heart. The punch of longing left her feeling breathless and conflicted again. Temper sparked as she made her exit. Was he *trying* to make her crazy? He'd agreed to this, agreed it was over—if not in words than by his actions. What right did he have to act like nothing was wrong?

Nate caught them during the change of scene. "Great job staying in character, you two. You've been struggling a bit the last couple of weeks, but you're really back on point."

In character, Tyler thought. *Of course. This isn't about messing with me, it's about the show. He's doing this for the show.*

Brody wasn't trying to push her into anything; he'd just dropped his guard with her to play the part.

The truth of that made her bleed again—again and again, she kept finding new ways to hurt. But she put the hurt aside. If Brody could do this for the Madrigal, so could she. This show would be her final performance. Once he left Wishful, nothing would get her on stage again, so it was important she give it her all.

So Tyler let the walls drop for the last time, and the old magic ignited.

She danced. She sang. And she fell in love with Phil Davis, while they schemed to matchmake Bob and Betty and rescue a retired general from obscurity. Brody glowed, owning the stage. Every smile, every glance seemed to be for her alone, despite the full house. It was their best performance ever. She didn't need Nate's delighted soft shoe at the transition to the final act to tell her that. Every touch of Brody's hand set off a spark in her blood.

When the final song began to play and he grabbed her for a kiss behind the center stage Christmas tree, she wasn't Judy Haynes and he wasn't Phil Davis. The arms that came around her held on, the lips that met hers tasted of the same pent up longing and need that had been torturing her for weeks. God, *God,* she'd missed him so much. She wanted to find a dark corner and drown in him. Myles' boot kicking Brody's leg was the only thing that kept them from missing their cue.

As "I've Got My Love To Keep Me Warm" spun out and the curtain calls began, Tyler struggled to rein in her emotions. The row of castmates in front filed out of the way, and Brody took her hand, leading her in a complicated dance that had the crowd hooting and cheering with approval. She couldn't hold back the joy or the pain as he spun her away for her bow. The audience's applause washed over her, making her feel at once soothed and triumphant. She'd done it. Whatever else could be said, she'd given this performance her all.

Straightening, Tyler turned back to take Brody's hand.

And found him down on one knee.

Everything inside her came to a jarring halt, and she almost stumbled. All the blood drained from her face, yet her cheeks felt almost scalding as she covered them with her hands. Beyond the stage, the cheers of the audience quieted into whispers. A sense of anticipation filled the air.

Brody's thumb brushed over the edge of a small box. "I've carried this around with me for a long time. It's been to the top of the Eiffel Tower and all across the country. But it was always meant to be here. Because this place, this stage, is central to what we are to each other."

This isn't happening, Tyler thought dully.

And yet the orchestra was changing its tune. Brody angled his head, a quizzical expression on his face until he recognized the music. Then he smiled.

It took a few more bars before Tyler's ears processed the melody. "All I Ask Of You."

"Oh, God," she whispered.

"I've known you most of my life," Brody continued. "You were the cute little blonde girl with pigtails, who spent her time building forts out of tree limbs during recess instead of playing kiss-chase like the other girls. The amazingly fast track star, who took the high school by storm. But it wasn't until I stood on this stage with you for *Oklahoma!* callbacks and heard you sing that I really looked at you. You took my breath away. I fell in love with you when I played Curly. And I did it all over again, every single time we sang, every time we danced.

"When I screwed things up, it was this theater that brought you back into my life. This show that gave me the chance to earn you back and show you that I never stopped loving you. And I screwed it up again. But I'm taking a leap here and hoping this will show you, in no uncertain terms, that I love you. Because you are my perfect match, in every way. So I'm asking you, Tyler Anne Edison, in front of our friends and cast members and this entire audience, to marry me and be the leading lady of my life." He flipped open the box, and the diamond inside flashed in the stage lights.

Tyler pressed a hand to her mouth, blinking against the tears. He was offering her everything she wanted…and yet.

"What about Portland?" she said, helplessly.

"It's temporary. I'm coming back home to Wishful. To you. If you'll have me."

I'm coming home.

No three words had ever sounded so wonderful. Tyler loosed a shuddering breath. "Thank *God.*"

Brody's lips twitched. "You have to say it," he said. "I want witnesses."

She laughed and pitched her voice so all could hear. "Yes, Brody Theodore Jensen, I will marry you."

"Then let's make it official." He pulled the ring out of the box and slid it on her finger. "I love you, Tyler."

Tyler framed his face in her hands. "I love you, Brody." Then she fisted a hand in his Santa jacket and jerked him to his feet, fusing her mouth to his while the crowd went wild.

❧

BREATHLESS, Brody staggered off the dance floor and accepted a fresh glass of champagne. The cast party turned engagement party at Speakeasy was in full swing, and he was pretty sure it was just as packed as karaoke night had been.

"Thank God tomorrow's performance isn't until seven."

"Amen," Tucker agreed, lifting his pilsner in a toast. "To friends, love, and gullibility."

Tyler lifted a brow. "What exactly is *that* supposed to mean?"

"That I can finally take this off," Tucker said. He bent over and unfastened the Velcro holding on his walking cast. "Thank God. This thing is so hot and itchy. I can't imagine what it's like for people who really did break their leg." He stepped out of the boot and toed off his remaining shoe, doing a happy little bounce and tap routine in his sock feet.

"What the hell, man?" Brody demanded.

Tyler's jaw had dropped. "Your leg wasn't broken?"

"Just a small, internal, muscular hemorrhage, sir," Tucker said, saluting. "I faked the whole thing so Brody would get promoted from understudy to Phil."

"You did what?" Brody laughed.

"You sneaky bastard," Tyler. "I brought you poppyseed chicken!"

Tucker patted his stomach. "And it was damned good poppyseed chicken."

Brody shifted his attention to Piper. "But you said it was broken. You took him to the ER yourself."

"I was in collusion," she said simply. "We figured if anything would get you two to work out your differences, it would be playing opposite each other again."

"So you pulled a Phil and Judy on Phil and Judy," he concluded.

"Pretty much." Tucker grinned, smug. He tapped his glass to Piper's.

"And our work here is done," she said.

"Imagine if they used their combined powers for evil," Brody said.

"Terrifying." Tyler raised her own glass. "To friends who knew better than we did, and most of all, to the Madrigal."

"To the Madrigal!"

~

Choose Your Next Romance!

Who do you want to see next in Wishful?

If you've got a nose for news, then you'll fall in love with newspaperman Myles Stewart, hero of Book 4, *Just For This Moment*. If you suspected shenanigans between him and Piper during the show, well, you were right! Fans of marriage of convenience tales are gonna LOVE this zany pair.

Keep turning the pages for *The Matchmaker Maneuver*, a prequel novelette that runs concurrent with *Be Careful, It's My Heart*.

After that, you can check out the first chapter of *Just For This Moment!*

THE MATCHMAKER MANEUVER

A WISHFUL PREQUEL

Myles Stewart had been driven by one, single aspiration since he was eight years old: Become Perry White. Upon the disappointing discovery that he could not, in fact, go work for *The Daily Planet*, he'd set his sights on *The New York Times. The Chicago Tribune. The Boston Globe.* His family had assumed he'd outgrow the desire and would fall in line with their expectations by the time he graduated college. They figured he'd tire of the life after he bounced from *The Times-Picayune* up to *The Seattle Times*, then over to *The Philadelphia Daily News*. But he never tired of the chase, of the quest to be the first in the know, of the pursuit of truth.

Then the bottom fell out of journalism. Every paper in the country experienced mass layoffs and downsizing. Realizing his days were probably numbered in Philly, Myles did something that baffled his big city colleagues. He came home to Mississippi and bought a struggling newspaper in a town where, his friends were convinced, absolutely nothing happened.

"Did you hear about the police chase in Lawley last week?"

"No. What happened?"

"This guy stole an ambulance and led them on a high speed

chase out of town. Got up to eighty-five miles an hour. While he was driving, he took his clothes off and tossed 'em right out the window. I'm not quite sure how it happened, but he ended up stopping at the Mount Zion Missionary Baptist Church and walking in during the service. He's buck nekkid, remember? The police tased him right there in the center aisle and took him to the nut house. Read it in the paper this morning."

"My Lord. What is the world coming to?"

Myles smiled to himself. That one had been particularly entertaining to follow up on.

Okay. So *The Wishful Observer* wasn't *The Daily Planet*. But unlike their metropolitan counterparts, small town newspapers were, according to some, still a viable market. So what if Warren Buffett couldn't pull it off? He wasn't a newspaperman. As owner/Editor-in-Chief, Myles intended to bring *The Observer* back from the brink, along with his whopping staff of three people, two of whom were part-time.

After two weeks on the job, Myles was willing to admit he might've bitten off a bit more than he'd meant to chew, but he loved nothing more than a challenge. Right now that challenge was rapidly immersing himself in the community in order to suss out his existing and potential audiences. So far that had meant multiple artery clogging breakfasts at Dinner Belles Cafe, where, praise God, he got his first properly cooked grits since he left for college.

"Your usual, sugar. Bowl of grits, two biscuits, and bacon." The waitress slid the plate in front of him.

Myles offered her a broad smile, delighted that he'd graduated to having a usual. "Thanks, Corinne."

"Can I top off that coffee for you?"

"Sure can." She leaned over to fill his mug.

"So what's your story?" he asked. In his two weeks coming in here, she'd been his waitress almost every day, and he'd formulated his own version of what he imagined her life was out of his observations. She worked in a greasy spoon, yet was painfully thin. A faint odor of cigarette smoke clung to her clothes. She was friendly with customers, downright flirtatious with the men, in a way that said she'd been used to male attention earlier in her life and expected it as her due. No rings. He was betting on former high school queen fallen on harder times. He wanted to know how much of it was right.

One carefully tweezed brow arched up. "My story?"

"Sure. Everybody's got one. What's yours?"

"Oh, nothin' that interesting."

"Everybody's interesting," Myles assured her.

"You've got me beat on that one, Mr. Big City Reporter. Lived all over and ended up here. I can't imagine why you'd want to do that."

"I wanted a different life. And good grits." He spooned up a bite of his. "Mmm."

"Well, we do have those. You enjoy now." She headed off to check her other tables.

As he worked his way through the grits, Myles tuned in to the other conversations around him.

"Have you *seen* the new ER doctor?" The woman behind him almost purred it.

"We have a new ER doc?"

"Dr. Chad Phillips. I had to take my grandmother in for chest pains—she was fine, by the way—and he was the one on duty. I swear, he could give me a breast exam any time."

Her companion snorted. "I thought you said he was an ER doc."

"They're supposed to be well-rounded."

Myles wondered if he could get the good doctor to agree to a profile piece introducing him to the community. From the sounds of it, if he were single, that might result in him being mobbed by all the unattached women in town. But maybe the guy could wangle an endless supply of casseroles and pies out of the deal.

The bell over the door rang. A balding man Myles pegged to be in his mid-forties came inside, a stack of papers in his hand. He skipped the meet-and-greet so common with other patrons and headed straight for the counter. The kitchen door swung open and Myles' favorite character ambled out. Mama Pearl Buckley was, he'd learned, queen of two things in this town—pie and gossip. Which was why he'd made Dinner Belles his informal bullpen. Almost nothing went on in Wishful without her knowing about it.

"What can I do for you, Nate?"

"I was hoping you'd put up a flier about auditions."

"Sure. What's the show this time?"

"*White Christmas*. And it may end up being our last."

"How's that?"

"The Madrigal is in hock up to its balconies. Mr. Stanton's kids started looking into things after he passed a few months ago and the whole thing's a mess. This show is our stay of execution. If we can raise enough, we might be able to save it."

"You know I'll help however I can." She accepted one of the fliers.

Myles slid from his booth and walked over. "Excuse me."

Both of them turned toward him.

"Hi. I couldn't help but overhear. I might be able to help a bit myself. I'm Myles Stewart, the new editor of *The Observer*. If you've got a few minutes to sit down with me, I'd love to run something in the paper to let the rest of the town know what's going on."

"That'd be great. Mama Pearl, can I get a cup of coffee since I'm staying?"

"Comin' right up."

The two men retreated to Myles' booth. Myles pulled a steno pad and pen from his messenger bag, prepared to take notes.

"So, tell me about the Madrigal. I gather it's a theater?"

"It is. Our community theater, over on Front Street. It was built back in 1912 as a home for vaudeville."

"Seriously? In a town this size?"

Nate shrugged. "Wishful has always been a home for the arts. They ran live productions until the start of World War II. There was a brief stretch where it was almost converted to a movie theater, but then Edward Stanton bought it in 1958. He performed the first restoration and expansion because he didn't believe that the people of Wishful should miss out on the arts just because it was small. Over the years, the Madrigal has earned a reputation as one of the best community theaters in the south. We've done everything from Shakespeare to Rogers and Hammerstein. I've been directing productions there for the past twenty years. It's a real part of town history. But, like so many things around here, it's seen better days."

"I understand Wishful's economy has been in a decline for the last couple of decades." Myles had seen back issues of the paper talking about it.

"Probably a bit longer. It's started to turn around under the leadership of the new city planner, but she's just one person and can only do so much. Our best shot is to put on a show that's sufficiently popular to bring in folks from the surrounding areas, raising enough revenues to pay off the debts enough to bring them current."

"How much will it take?"

Nate named a figure that had Myles whistling. "Damn. You've got your work cut out for you." He hoped like hell the actors in this community theater were better than most of the community level shows he'd seen. "*The Observer* is happy to help however it can. I'll be happy to write a human interest piece to go in the next edition, as well as announcing auditions. Do you think you could make time later today to meet me and my staff photographer for a quick little tour? A pic of the stage would make for good front page imagery."

Nate slid from the booth. "I can do that. Around three-thirty?"

"We'll be there."

"I appreciate your help, Mr. Stewart."

"Myles, please."

"Myles then."

"I'll do what I can to connect everybody to the plight of the Madrigal—whether they're into theater or not. Really give them a feel for what they'd be missing if it closed its doors."

"It's a good start," said Nate, heading for the door, "but the only way to truly experience the theater is from the stage."

"HAVE YOU SEEN *THE Observer* this morning?"

Piper Parish took a well-deserved two-minute break, dropping into a chair beside Shelby Abbott, the clinic office manager. They'd had a rush of stomach flu and the start of a scabies outbreak from the moment the doors opened at eight, and Piper's dogs were starting to bark, even in the orthopedic shoes. "No, why?"

Shelby passed it over, tapping the front page.

Historic Madrigal Theater To Close?

"*What?*" Piper bent over the newspaper and devoured the article. "Oh, no no no no. This is terrible!"

The Madrigal was her second home. She'd grown up there. So many of her memories were tied up with that place, Piper couldn't fathom it closing its doors or, worse, being turned into something else entirely.

"Looks like all hope isn't lost. They're doing a last ditch show of *White Christmas*," Shelby pointed out.

If they were going to save the theater from financial ruin with this one last production, they needed to pull out all the stops. "Tyler has to come out of retirement for auditions."

Shelby stared Piper down over the rims of her glasses. "You can't be serious."

"You know nobody in town can dance like she can."

"It's been eight years."

"Have you thought about what this could do to her?"

Piper felt a prick of guilt. There were very good reasons Tyler hadn't set foot on stage in the better part of a decade. But it was the right thing. It had to be. Tyler needed this as much as the Madrigal did. For closure.

"It's not going to be *traumatic*. I've got a heart, for God's sake. It'll be good for her to get back on the stage and remember how much fun we used to have. She's moved on." Or she would, if she went through with the show.

"I hope you're right," Shelby said and turned back to their next patient.

Another two hours and most of a bottle of hand sanitizer passed before Piper could shake free for her lunch break. She raced across town to Edison Hardware, buoyed by an optimism that Tyler wouldn't let the specter of one Brody Jensen keep her from doing her part to save the theater. She could see Tyler through the door, ringing somebody up. Shoving inside, she announced, "Dust off your dancing shoes, we have a mission."

Tyler didn't even pause in giving her instructions to Mrs. Van Buren.

Okay, going to be a tough sell.

The older woman grinned. "This is going to look so good! I'll be sure to take pictures."

"You do that. Be sure to tag us on Facebook!" Tyler called.

"I will!"

As soon as Mrs. Van Buren was out of the shop, Piper hopped up on the counter and swung her legs. "Did you hear what I said?"

With a bland stare, Tyler began stocking cabinet hardware. "I'm pretty sure you're the only one who remembers I ever *wore* dancing shoes."

Piper hated that Tyler had given up something she loved so much. "Not the truth and so not the point."

"And what *is* the point? You know I don't dance anymore."

"You will for this. The Madrigal is in danger."

Tyler paused, a drawer pull in her hand and that hesitation gave Piper hope. "That's terrible! But what does it have to do with me?"

"They've agreed to let us make one last effort to raise the money to save it. To prove that it can be a sound investment. Nate is directing a production of *White Christmas*. And you're going to unearth your dancing shoes from whatever graveyard you left them in to audition for it with me."

"You used to dance?" Norah Burke, the new city planner, spoke up from her seat at the project table.

"I haven't danced or sung since college."

Piper hopped down and pointed an accusatory finger. "You lie. You've sung and danced with me as recently as last month."

"What we do in the privacy of my living room under the influence of a pitcher of margaritas is between you and me and no one else. And wipe that considering smirk off your face, Norah."

"What smirk?"

"The one that says you're trying to figure out how you can use that in your next community development scheme." She shoved plastic wrapped hardware into the Plexiglas bins.

"Oh, come on, Tyler," Piper insisted. "It's not like you've lost your chops. You'd be a shoe-in for Judy. And I would make the perfect Betty."

"Give me one good reason why I should come out of retirement."

Piper's lips twitched. "Let's just say, we're doing it for a pal in the Army."

One hand fisted on her hip, Tyler leveled a Look in her direction.

Unabashed, she shrugged. "What? It was appropriate. We're

doing it in the name of the good old days. Think of how many great memories we have of the Madrigal. Our first show. Our first lead roles. My first kiss with Robert Hudson in *Meet Me In St. Louis*. Where you first fell in love with—" Piper cut herself off. *Nope, do not go there.* "Okay, so maybe that one's not good to remind you about, but you can't hold his asshatishness against the Madrigal."

"Whose asshatishness?" Norah asked

"He who will not be named," Piper intoned, with a look that told Norah she'd tell all at the first opportunity. Away from Tyler.

"I'm not holding anything against the Madrigal," Tyler said. Her expression shifted to resignation before Piper could say *prove it*. "When are auditions?"

"Tonight at six."

"Tonight! Piper, I've got to close. I've got nothing to wear here and no time to go home and get my shoes, not to mention I've got nothing prepared for an audition."

"So tell me where your shoes are and what you want, and I'll go by and pick everything up for you."

"I still don't have anything prepared."

"Oh *come on*. As if you can't sing every single number from the show in your sleep." The pair of them had done sing-a-long viewings of the movie for the last twenty years.

"It's not the singing part that has me worried."

"Tyler," Piper drew out the plea to five syllables and folded her hands in prayer, complete with the puppy dog eyes that had, over the years, successfully convinced Tyler to go skydiving, be in a bachelorette auction for a hospital fundraiser, and add a set of very purple, very unfortunate highlights to her blonde hair.

Tyler scowled. "You don't fight fair."

"It's the *Madrigal*."

"Fine. I'll be there, but I'll be a little late. We don't close until six."

Piper knew when to take her victory and run. "Fabulous! I'll meet you there with your shoes and your outfit. Where are they?"

Tyler sighed. "Top shelf of my closet, in the blue box."

Piper gave a squee and wrapped Tyler in a rib-cracking hug. "I'll meet you there! Bye, Norah." Without another word, she whirled and bounced out the door. She had just enough time to pick up Tyler's shoes before heading back to work.

THE MADRIGAL WAS a glorious old place. The kind of theater that told a story besides the ones being played out on the stage. As he stepped into the auditorium, Myles looked around, taking in the delightfully ostentatious woodwork and all the tiny touches remaining from an era when craftsmanship still meant something. Man, they didn't make them like this anymore. What a delightful surprise to find somewhere like this in his newly adopted hometown.

A woman on the stage was running through "Count Your Blessings Instead of Sheep". A more than passable rendition, he decided. At least on par with what he expected for community theater. He saw Nate settled a few rows back from the front, in prime position to watch all the action. Having no wish to interrupt, Myles headed about halfway down the aisle himself and slid into one of the plush velvet seats. He slid a notebook out of his messenger bag and began jotting down impressions of the building, observations of the hopeful players scattered around the room.

A door to his left opened, and a woman slipped out, quiet as a shadow.

Hello gorgeous.

She wore one of those dance costume things that looked like a swimsuit with a long flowy skirt. A leotard? The skirt trailed behind her like the tail of a comet as she moved up the side aisle. She was clearly on a mission, looking for someone or something.

From the stage, somebody launched into a painfully off-key rendition of "Blue Skies". Ignoring that poor guy, Myles twisted in his seat to watch the woman progress toward the back. Had she already auditioned? Before the question even finished forming, she'd come back from the lobby, headed back toward the door to the stage.

Up front, Nate quietly conversed with the "Count Your Blessings" chick. As the ear torture ended, she rose and headed up the aisle. Myles called out softly as she came by, "Hey, nice audition."

She stopped. "Thanks. Are you auditioning?"

"Hadn't thought about it. I'm here doing a story for the paper. Have you got a minute to chat with me?"

"Sure." She dropped into a chair beside him. "I'm Charlotte Ballard."

"Myles Stewart. So is this your first audition or have you done this for a while?"

"Definitely not my first. I've been doing community theater off and on for about four years now. A lot of the folks here tonight have been in it a lot longer than that."

"Yeah?"

"The Madrigal is important around here. Once the word hit the grapevine that it was in danger, the pressure was on to get the best of the best to auditions. Take this guy." She nodded to indicate a blond guy that replaced the off-key gentleman.

"I'm Tucker McGee, and I'll be auditioning for the role of Phil."

"What're you singing, Tucker?" Nate asked.

"'Happy Holidays.'"

The music started and Tucker launched into the number.

Charlotte dropped her voice. "He's been doing this since he was a kid. He's part of the Old Guard talent."

Tucker was good. His vocal tone and expression were

completely on point, and more importantly, he could move. Like, Danny Kaye himself kind of rhythm.

"Color me impressed," Myles murmured.

"Tucker is guaranteed to be Phil. He's been the lead for anything requiring dancing for...well, ever it seems like."

Another woman passed Myles on the inside aisle, moving with slow deliberation toward the stage door, an expression caught somewhere between nostalgia and dread. There was a story there. There was, he suspected, a story for a great many of the people auditioning tonight. Individual connections to the Madrigal.

"Oh!" Charlotte exclaimed softly, laying a hand on Myles' arm to draw his attention to the woman in the aisle. "Now *this* is interesting. That's Tyler Edison. She hasn't been on stage in eight years but she used to be *amazing*. Nobody in town can dance like her."

"Eight years, huh? I thought you said you'd only been doing this for four."

"I have. But I'm a local. Around here, Tyler is legend."

"Has she been gone?"

"Oh no, she runs the hardware store. It's been in her family for generations."

"So why the long hiatus?"

"The whole thing was really sad. She was half of the community theater power couple. From the time they were seventeen, if there was a love story, they were the leads. Which was easy for them because they were crazy about each other, so most of it wasn't acting. Everybody figured they'd get married after college."

"I gather that dream went poof."

"Both his parents were killed in a car crash. He just wasn't right after that. One day he just up and left her, without a word. Never came back to Wishful. Tyler hasn't been on stage since. Too painful, I guess."

"Apparently the theater is more important than heartbreak."

Perspective of the players, he thought, making another note about doing a series of interviews with each of the final cast members to give that human touch for what the theater meant to them.

"Just you wait. She's going to be amazing," Charlotte assured him.

Myles didn't have to wait long before Tyler came out to center stage, Miss Gorgeous on her heels. The pair of them held cardboard fans and sported identical grins.

"Tyler Edison." Myles could hear the smile in Nate's voice. "Well, it's about damn time you came back. Good to see you."

Tyler lifted her hand in a wave.

"I guess I don't have to ask which number you two are doing," he said. "Go on then."

The music cued up and they launched in to "Sisters". Myles forgot he was just watching auditions, so clearly did the two women slide into the roles of Betty and Judy Haynes. The gorgeous brunette played a fabulous Betty, and he found himself wishing for a Phil to banter with over her brown eyes.

When the number was over, Betty gave Tyler a high five. "Nailed it."

Tyler answered with a hip bump. "We've still got it."

If Nate didn't cast those two as the female leads, he was insane. They were perfect.

Myles thought about what the director had said, that the only way to really experience the theater was from the stage. Dancing wasn't his strong suit, but he had a pretty decent voice that he tended to use only in the shower or on long road trips. If he jumped in and auditioned for Bob, he might get a chance to read with his Betty. Not that he expected to actually get the part, but it'd be worth the effort just for a chance to meet her.

"So if I decided to actually audition, who do I need to talk to about that?"

Charlotte pointed at Nate. "Just tell the director. He'll put you on the list."

Mind made up, Myles slid out of his seat and went to talk to Nate.

～

"Hey, who's that new guy sitting with Tucker?"

From stage left, Piper followed Tyler's gaze to the card table set up center stage for a reading of the scene in Novello's where the Haynes sisters first meet Wallace and Davis. The prospective Bob was a bit leaner than Tucker, but just as tall. Brown hair a couple of shades darker than her own flopped endearingly into his eyes, giving him an appealing look that was saved from being too boyish by the clean angles of his jaw. "I don't know, but he's cute!"

"Don't get any ideas," Tyler groused.

As if she'd be stupid enough to try to match-make Tyler with some strange guy. She had her limits. "Not for you, for me."

"He's not one of my customers. Maybe he's new or from one of the surrounding towns?"

New or nearby were both completely acceptable options in Piper's mind. In a town of five thousand, the dating pool tended to be shallow, so the arrival of new eligible bachelors merited checking out. Which was terribly Austenesque, but such was the reality of dating in a small town. "Well, I guess we'll find out in a bit."

They waited for their cue to join the boys.

Piper snaked her hand out to grab Tyler's and squeezed. "I'm glad you came out tonight."

Tyler tipped her head to Piper's shoulder and sighed softly. "Me too. It wasn't as bad as I thought it might be."

Oh thank God. Piper had been terrified that she'd made some mistake forcing Tyler into this. "Good. I want to save the Madrigal, but not at the expense of legitimately hurting you."

"I'm not that breakable anymore."

Piper had her doubts about that.

"That's our cue," Tyler said.

Saved by the script.

Piper slid into character as they approached the table, adding a layer of restrained propriety to her usual manner as she introduced herself and her "sister" before taking a seat.

Unlike the others, she and Tyler didn't have scripts in their hands. Given Nate had pulled the dialogue straight from the movie, they didn't need any. Bob didn't seem to need to check his often and his aggrieved expression toward Tucker as Phil suggested he had a solid familiarity with the source material himself. Points for him, she decided.

As Tucker-Phil and Tyler-Judy got up to go dance, Piper fixed an earnest expression on her face, prepared to come clean.

"You know, I was so surprised to get that letter from Benny," Bob said.

"Mr. Wallace, I'm afraid you've been brought here under false pretenses."

Bob watched her as she went through the explanation, outlining Judy's deception. His eyes—which were a lovely shade of caramel brown, fringed by those long lashes so often wasted on guys—fired in challenge and amusement as they verbally sparred, scooting their chairs closer together. They were completely in sync, fixed in the roles, which was the best kind of stage chemistry to have. It made the role less like acting and more like just living under really bright lights.

"Mr. Wallace, since the chances of our seeing each other again is extremely remote, I don't think it's important to go on arguing."

"I'll drink to that," Bob said, and laid his hand over hers.

Piper felt the zing all the way down to her toes. *Maybe not just stage chemistry.*

"Good!" Nate's praise from the auditorium floor shattered the moment, making it too weird to flip her hand over to lace with his, which she could've blamed on the part if the director hadn't spoken.

Bob let her go and rose as she did, while the next quartet got set up to read. He followed Piper into the wings.

"That was well done," she told him. "Are you a *White Christmas* fan?"

"It's my sister's favorite Christmas movie, so it's been part of the holiday rotation forever. I'm Myles by the way." He smiled at her, and Piper felt a pleasant flutter in her belly.

Nerves? This guy was making her nervous? Holy crap, when was the last time that had happened?

"Piper."

"So are you new or part of the Old Guard?" Myles asked. At her questioning look, he said, "I was chatting with Charlotte earlier. She mentioned a lot of the people coming out tonight were long-running players in WCT productions."

"Oh, well, yes. I grew up in this theater. I've been acting since elementary school."

"Not surprised. I figure you're a shoe-in for Betty."

Piper was inclined to agree, but it wasn't the kind of thing you said out loud. It was both rude and bad luck. "What about you? I know you're new in town."

His brows lifted. "Do I have a sign?"

She grinned. "You're either new in town or you have the best immune system this side of Jackson."

"Huh?"

"I'm a nurse. If you'd lived in Wishful any real length of time, you'd have eventually rotated through my clinic. Everyone does."

"Oh." He gave a self-deprecatory laugh. "Yeah, guilty as charged. I've only been here about two and a half weeks. Still finding my footing in the community."

There'd been no ring on his finger during the reading, but some people might've taken it off to stay in character. She wasn't about to come right out and ask.

"Are you new to theater?"

"I am. This is, in fact, my first audition ever."

Piper felt a pang of disappointment. He'd done well, no question, but for this show they needed the absolute best of the best, and that meant an actor with more experience. Too bad. She'd have enjoyed playing Betty to his Bob.

As the second quartet finished the reading, Nate hollered for her to come back out as part of a new group. She shot Myles a flirtatious smile. "Duty calls. Welcome to Wishful, Myles. I hope to see you around."

"Count on it," he called after her.

She held in the instinctive fist pump and took her place on stage.

HE'D WON THE LEAD. Myles was reasonably sure no one was more shocked about it than him. His whim had just claimed his nights and weekends for the next three months. But given those nights and weekends would be spent playing opposite the lovely Piper Parish, he couldn't find much reason to complain. He'd wanted to get to know her. Hell, as Bob to her Betty, he'd even get to kiss her. Were stage kisses different from real kisses? He didn't know. But, he looked forward to learning.

The auditorium was full of cast, crew, and musicians, all overflowing with an infectious, effervescent optimism. The general mood made him feel like whistling a tune and executing a little dance step as he strode up the center aisle toward the stage. Not that he really knew any dance steps outside the waltz, foxtrot, cha cha, and swing, and he wasn't sure how much he'd retained since eighth grade. Cotillion didn't exactly prepare one for this brand of choreography. But as Bob, he didn't have that much dancing to do. That was all on Tucker McGee. He and Tyler were already executing some kind of complicated dance move on one side of the stage.

Piper strode out from one of the wings. *Stage right*, Myles reminded himself. Part of doing this was learning the right lingo. He headed up on stage via the orchestra pit stairs, trying to decide whether to shoot for nonchalance or I'm-a-newb-please-help-me-navigate-unfamiliar-waters.

She looked up as he approached and whatever clever thing he might've said bled right out of his brain.

"Hi." *Oh brilliant, Stewart. Way to impress the girl.*

"So you survived auditions," she said. "Congratulations."

"Thanks. It was…unexpected. But I'm excited. Glad to be here. Hopefully you can share your greater experience and keep me from mucking anything up."

But Piper wasn't paying attention to him anymore. Silence fell around them. Myles looked around for the reason, thinking maybe Nate had come in and the actors were going automatically silent out of respect or something. Across the stage, Tyler had stopped, having obviously just come out of a turn. She stared at something in the back of the auditorium. As the silence stretched out, more of the cast seemed to follow her example. Myles looked toward the back, seeing a guy standing just inside the lobby doors. He seemed suspended, waiting for something. The waves of tension between the newcomer and Tyler were almost strong enough to push Myles back a step. This had to be the heartbreaker Charlotte told him about.

The floorboards of the stage popped, and the tableau unfroze.

Finding out the details about what the hell was going on seemed like a good excuse to keep talking to Piper. Before he could make an attempt, Nate requested an attention grabber on the piano. The pianist banged out a little riff, calling rehearsal to order.

"…choreographer will be here on Friday, so the name of the game this week is to learn all your music and start learning your lines. The schedule is in your script packets." Nate picked one up, waved it. "Now, if any of you are familiar with the actual stage production of *White Christmas The Musical*, you will know that it bears little resemblance to the movie we all know and love. I chose this show based on nostalgia. *White Christmas* is my favorite Christmas movie, and it's incredibly well-known. People hear we're putting on a production, *that's* the story they expect to see. So I contacted the Irving Berlin estate and requested permission to make my own adaptation of the movie script. Given we are a town of less than five thousand, they don't have a lot of fear this will become a raging success, so they actually said yes. That said, it's a one shot deal. We get one three week run of the show, and that's that. Permanently retired after that. But at least we'll be adhering as faithfully as possible to the actual plot and script of the movie, with minor changes to facilitate our set limitations. So come and get 'em and let's get started."

Myles headed to the back of the line, intending to position himself beside Piper, the better to pick her brain.

She stood close to Tucker, her voice low. "We have to do something. We'll never pull off the show if Tyler isn't at the top of her game."

Instead of butting into their conversation, Myles hung back, shamelessly eavesdropping, which was a reporter's default setting.

"What exactly do you propose we do? Brody's back after all this time. He's got as much right to be here as any of us," Tucker said.

She gave him a withering look. "We'll agree to disagree on that."

"It should be fine. He's just my understudy. I can run interference, keep them separated, if need be."

"To keep this from being a blood-letting, that might be wise."

The two of them looked across the stage to where the guy—Brody presumably—was attempting to talk to Tyler in the line. Myles could practically see clouds of condensed air rolling off her for all the luck the guy was having. His writer brain began churning. No question, this was the guy who'd broken Tyler's heart. And she was all kinds of pissed to be seeing him again.

Potential scenarios flew through his head, how he'd construct the story, what kind of ending he'd expect. Would Wishful be getting a show within a show? Given the way small towns seemed to operate and the fact that people still remembered what had happened close to a decade later, it seemed like a good possibility. Not that he'd be airing their personal conflicts in the paper—he was a journalist, not a gossip columnist. But he couldn't stop wondering whether Tyler and Brody would be able to put aside their personal crap in the name of saving the theater, or if Tyler would bail, leaving the role of Judy to her understudy Charlotte.

Time would tell.

IN ALL HER years living in Wishful, Piper had never actually been to the offices of *The Wishful Observer*. She'd seen the doors, of course, facing Oxford Street, but she'd never had reason to go inside or even much wonder about the people who worked there. She read the paper like everybody else and just kind of accepted that it would come out when it came out—which, the last few years, was three times a week. But now she had a face attached to the paper. A very nice face she'd been running lines with for two weeks now. And she was curious. She was also on a mission.

An older woman looked up as Piper stepped inside. "Can I help you?"

"I'm looking for Myles."

"He's on the phone just now, but if you want to take a seat just over there, you'll be able to see him when he gets off." She gestured to a small waiting area across from a glass wall.

Piper thanked her and sat. Myles moved beyond the glass, pacing around his desk with some kind of headset on, a Slinky rolling from hand to hand as he talked. She wasn't sure what she'd expected the office of a newspaper editor to look like, but his wasn't it. A variety of toys sat around the room. More things like the Slinky that he could play with while he thought. Framed posters of comic book women lined one wall. Not the over-sexed, busty kind she'd seen in her cousin's comic books, but sharp, smart-looking women. She wondered who they were.

Myles himself was a strange contradiction, in an untucked, French-cuffed button-down and jeans. Deliberate or the product of a failure to do laundry? God, he was adorkable. He put her in mind of a much younger, much sexier Perry White. Not that she needed to find her costar sexy. Sexy absolutely wasn't the name of the game with Betty and Bob. They were wholesome. But as she watched, he leaned over to look at something on a computer screen, slipping a pair of horn-rimmed reading glasses on. Piper's mouth watered. Oh, she had a real soft spot for the sexy geek look. Very Jude Law from *The Holiday*.

Myles finished his call and removed the headset and glasses, tossing both in the midst of the piles of paper on his desk and running a hand through his thick, dark hair. Catching sight of her, his serious expression shifted to a smile, and he crossed to open the door. "Well this is a pleasant surprise. Come on in."

"Thanks. I read your article in the paper this morning. The interview with Barbara Monahan. It was really poignant."

"I'm working on a series of interviews with various members of the cast. I want to really bring home to the community how much the Madrigal means to people."

"I think it's a great idea." She dropped into a chair opposite his desk as he leaned back against the front of it. "I really appreciate what you're trying to do here. Especially since you're new to Wishful."

"Good journalism is about people, about community, and I took over the paper here because I wanted to be at the heart of a good one."

Dozens of questions rolled through her brain. Personal stuff better suited to a date than a business meeting. But she wasn't quite ready to get down to business. Instead she smiled and jerked her head toward the posters on the wall. "Who are they?"

"My inspirations. That's Lois Lane, Brenda Starr, and Vicki Vale."

"Okay, Lois Lane I know. Who are the other two?"

"They're all kick ass female reporters from the comic world. Lois from *Superman*, obviously. Brenda had her own comic series, and Vicki is from *Batman*."

Piper angled her head. "Why them instead of, say, Perry White or that editor guy from *Spiderman*? The one with the mustache?"

Myles grinned. Damn but he had a great smile. "J. Jonah Jameson. Well, for one, the ladies are more fun to look at. And for another, they were the ones who put their butts on the line to get out there and report the truth. I find that more appealing than just sitting behind a desk."

"And is getting out from behind the desk why you decided to audition? Nate said you had come that night just for a story." That was edging into the personal again, but she couldn't help herself.

"Well, partly. I did decide that telling the story from the perspective of one of the performers would be another way to engage people. But honestly? I wanted to meet you."

Piper blinked, surprise and pleasure diffusing her cheeks with warmth. "That's...flattering."

"I don't want to overstep any boundaries or make something weird. Are you seeing anybody?"

She wasn't quite sure what to think about his candor. "No, I'm not. But you should know, I have a rule."

"A rule?"

"I don't date my costars."

He didn't look perturbed. "Why's that?"

"A couple reasons. For one, the show comes first. If you start dating your romantic lead and everything goes south, it's a lot harder to sell the part. I'm not going to do anything to endanger the quality of this show."

"Fair point. And the other reason?"

"Acting as romantic leads tends to engender a false sense of intimacy. The nature of the roles often means you fall into feelings of a relationship without going through the right order of things. So, you may start seeing each other during the show, keep seeing each other after, and then find out that what you thought was real attraction ends up being just a part you played that became familiar."

"That sounds like the voice of experience."

"Oh, it is. I have been burned before. So, while I'm incredibly flattered and not a little intrigued by your interest, I'm not going to pursue it while we're acting together." It was as direct and soft a put down as she could manage.

She expected a flicker of irritation or something. Instead he asked, "Do you have a waiting period?"

"A waiting period?"

"Sure. If you think there's false intimacy or whatever, do you have some standard waiting period for after the show is over to let it wear off? Because, if you do, I'd like to mark it on my calendar."

"Seriously?" she laughed.

"I'm nothing if not dogged in pursuit of the things that interest me."

"I can see that." The frank interest combined with the easy way he respected her boundaries made him all kinds of appealing. And that had her wanting to break her own rules. Before she could go down that path, she said, "Three months."

"So, three months after the show closes, you'd entertain the idea of going out with me?"

"Sure."

He picked up his phone. "Siri, remind me three months from December 20th to call Piper up for a date."

"Okay, I'll remind you."

Piper couldn't hold back the grin. "You're incorrigible. I shouldn't find that appealing."

"I'm just gonna put it out there that if you change your mind, I have no such rules."

"Noted."

He pushed away from the desk and circled around behind it. "So, since you obviously didn't come here for purposes of charm or seduction, what can I do for you?"

Piper pushed the flirt aside and pulled out the ad copy for the show. Time to get down to business.

"WHAT'LL YOU HAVE?" Myles asked.

"Anything," Piper replied.

"Well, tell me what you want to dream about, and I'll know what to give you."

The pause stretched out as Myles waited for her to return the line. "Oh, what's that?" she asked.

His Betty's brain was not at all on the task at hand. She kept glancing out at the loading dock, where Tucker and Brody were horsing around, fencing with PVC pipe and egging each other on in assorted accents. Did she have a thing for Tucker? Maybe he was the reason she had that rule about not dating your costars. Certainly he'd been around the theater almost as long as she had. But Myles simply hadn't gotten that vibe between them.

"I got a whole big theory about it. Different kind of food makes for different kind of dreams. Now, if you have a ham and cheese on rye, you'll dream about a tall, cool blonde. Peanut butter and jelly, you get a nice comfortable, average Joe. And a turkey on wheat with barbeque potato chips sandwiched in will get you a shape-shifting marmoset from Pluto."

Not even a flicker of response.

"It's a little chilly in here, isn't it?" she returned.

Yep, that confirmed it. Head totally not in the game.

As Myles started to speak, he caught a flash of Tucker leaping off the loading dock in some kind of spin kick.

"Tucker!" Piper screamed and raced to where he now lay, curled in a ball, arms wrapped protectively around his leg, swearing a blue streak.

Myles was right behind.

Piper crouched down, voice brisk and efficient. "Let me see."

Red-faced and faintly breathless, Tucker didn't want to unbend. "It hurts. Christ, it hurts."

"What happened?" Nate demanded, coming out from the stage doors.

"We were just fooling around," Tucker groaned. "Doing spin kicks off the back of the truck."

Tyler crouched on his other side, rubbing his back in a soothing gesture. "You *are* aware you aren't twenty-one anymore?"

"Brody can still do it."

Over Tucker's head, Tyler fixed Brody with a glare that placed all the blame squarely on him.

He held his hands up in a *How could I have known?* gesture.

"It's broken," Piper announced. "I can feel the bump in the bone."

"It can't be broken," Tucker argued. "I have to dance." He tried to stand, using Brody and Piper to lever himself up. But the moment he put weight on it, the leg buckled and he howled.

"Get him in my back seat," Piper ordered. "I'll take him to the emergency room."

"I don't wanna to go the ER."

"Then you shouldn't have broken your leg on a Saturday," she said practically.

Tucker looked miserably at Nate. "Sorry. I would never have tried it if I didn't think I could pull it off."

Nate scrubbed both hands over his red and gray beard, as if he could somehow rewind the last few minutes. "It's all right. You just get yourself taken care of. This is why we have understudies."

Tyler went pale at that.

"Somebody take him. I'll go get my car."

Myles stepped in. "Here, let me." He swapped positions with Piper, taking Tucker's weight.

She scurried down the alley.

"You want to sit down?" Brody asked.

"If I go down, you'll just have to haul me back up. It's not so bad as long as I'm not putting pressure on it."

"You can thank the adrenaline for that," Myles told him. "It'll hurt like a sonofabitch later."

"Personal experience?" Tucker asked.

Piper backed her car down the alley.

"Ski accident back in college. High point was the ski bunnies who felt compelled to entertain me the rest of the week since I was lodge-bound."

Tucker laughed. "Perhaps some of our cast members will take pity."

"It won't be me," Piper told him, opening the door to the back seat. "Idiots don't get special caretaking."

But her hands were careful as she, along with Myles and Brody, managed to get him into the seat.

"We'll all sign your cast, man," Brody told him.

"No profane drawings," Tucker ordered. "I'm an attorney. I've got a reputation to uphold."

"Aw, where's the fun in that?" Brody teased.

Regret and concern flickered over Piper's face as she glanced over at Tyler. "We'll keep you posted."

"Just take care of him," Tyler said.

As soon as the alley was clear, Nate hollered, "Let's get this truck unloaded."

The rest of the cast members, who'd been hanging around the

loading dock watching the drama unfold, sprang into motion again.

"Thank God it happened early so we're not having to pull a substitution right before opening night," said Nate, heading back inside.

Myles could see the indecision on Tyler's face. She wanted to quit. And, really, Myles kinda couldn't blame her. Piper had been right about the intimacy engendered by playing love interests in a show. To do that with someone who used to be an actual love interest had to be tough.

Her shoulders squared up, her eyes hardening. Decision made then.

Good for you, Myles thought.

Brody crossed over to her on the loading dock. "I've never seen him miss the landing before."

"A lot's changed in the last eight years," she said. "Tucker's not quite as spry as he used to be."

She wasn't talking about Tucker. Brody obviously knew it and was wise enough not to comment.

"Truck's empty," said Nate. "Let's get to rehearsal."

Brody gestured toward the stairs, a sweeping, courteous motion. "After you, Miss Haynes."

So it was to be a show in a show after all. Bringing up the rear, Myles hesitated at the threshold, thinking back to Tucker's fall. Piper had screamed before he ever hit the ground, almost as if she knew he was going to get hurt.

"—UNLESS I was to get myself engaged or something real fast," Tyler said.

"Yeah but where you gonna find somebody way out here?" Brody asked.

The lines were right but the body language for the scene was all wrong. Instead of snuggling up next to him as she tried to convince her "Phil" that he was the best candidate, Tyler looked like she wished she was on Mars.

"Cut!" shouted Nate.

Obviously, Piper wasn't the only one noting the problem. She gnawed her lip wondering if this would get better or if she'd made a huge miscalculation.

"Piper."

She turned toward Myles and realized it wasn't the first time he'd said her name. They were supposed to be running lines in the wings, and she was falling down on her part in a spectacular fashion. She turned her back to the stage and put her attention fully on her co-star. "I'm sorry. I'm sorry."

"You've been awfully distracted the past week."

"I know. I suck. I'll be better, I promise."

Instead of exasperation, he offered her a smirk. "You know, you might have a better time running your lines if you weren't busy plotting interference with your best friend's love life."

She froze, her heart giving a panicked lurch. Only years of training to speak calmly despite nerves kept her voice from shaking. "What?"

He crossed his arms and gave her a *busted* look. "I know what you and Tucker did."

Casting a fast look around to see that they were alone, Piper yanked him into a prop closet and shut the door. Of course, that closed them in to blackness. "Dammit, where's the light?"

She began to pat the walls around the door, aware of Myles shifting against who knew what behind her. She heard the sound of metal scraping ceramic as he found the pull chain and turned on the anemic bulb above them.

He should've looked ridiculous, standing there with a fake palm tree at his back and the tentacles from a purple foam octopus dangling above his head. Instead he looked just a little bit dangerous with that *oh you're in trouble now* expression.

"Why would you think Tucker and I did anything?" she demanded.

"Well, the fact that you dragged me in here for something other than making out like teenagers kind of screams guilt. I was guessing before, but you just confirmed my suspicions."

Piper cursed her impulsivity. But maybe this was still salvageable. "What is it you think we did?"

"You're pulling a Phil and Judy on Phil and Judy. Handy that you're a nurse. Did you bring anybody else in on things or did you put the cast on yourself?"

Oh God. Oh God, he really had figured it out. "But...how did you...?"

"I'm an investigative reporter by training, sweetheart. And as good an actress as you are on stage, subterfuge isn't your forte."

Oh no. Did Tyler suspect? No, surely not. She wouldn't hesitate to come kick Piper's ass into the next county if she knew. Another spurt of panic kicked her into motion. She flew at Myles, pressing him back against the palm tree. "You can't tell a soul. This is too important."

"Is it important for the show or important for your friend?"

Frustration bubbled. "Both." He didn't know the history, couldn't understand what this was really about.

"And exactly how does that fit in with that personal code of yours? You told me you wouldn't do anything to endanger the show. And I'm thinking this setup is a ticking time bomb of potential nasty."

He wasn't wrong. Watching for signs of disaster was why she'd been absolute crap with learning her part. "You don't understand," she insisted.

"You're right. I don't. But I'll give you a chance to plead your case over dinner."

Surely she hadn't heard him right. "Dinner?"

"At my place," he continued, "so we won't risk being overheard, since that's a concern for you."

"You're blackmailing me?"

"Technically this is extortion." The bastard had the nerve to offer a cheeky grin. "So what's it going to be? Dinner or do I blow this whole thing sky high?"

"You'd seriously march out there right now and tell them?"

"What do you think?"

Piper stared at him. That was the thing. She didn't know whether he'd do it or not because she didn't know him. Not really. She'd very carefully kept her distance since that day in his office, to try to limit her own temptation. She wanted to think he wasn't monster enough to expose her treachery—and Tyler would see it as treachery, no question—but she wasn't willing to call his bluff to find out. He had a helluva poker face. "Oh for God's sake. Dinner. Then at least I'll get the chance to explain."

"Okay then. Tomorrow night? After the afternoon rehearsal?"

"Fine." She'd just chew her nails down to nubs in the meantime.

"I'll cook," he said.

Could he cook? Piper decided it didn't matter either way. It wasn't likely she'd feel much like eating once she got through telling the tale.

"Deal." She meant to offer her hand to shake on it but realized that it was pressed to his chest. Apparently had been since she'd shoved him back against the palm tree. She started to jerk it back, but he covered her hand with his, holding it in place.

"Deal."

Jesus Christ, this closet was really freaking tiny, and they were really freaking close. Was he radiating all that heat or was it her?

Myles' lips curved into a devilish smile. "You wanna keep running lines from in here?"

"What?" Dammit, her voice was breathless.

"I mean, it's nice and cozy and all, but I expect we'll be missed before long. Unless you're into the making out like teenagers part. I'm completely amenable to that, show be damned."

Piper snatched her hand away and stumbled back. "You're impossible." But she was forced to admit, as she snuck back out of the closet, he was also very, very tempting.

~

BACK RAMROD STRAIGHT Piper marched past Myles into his living room and tossed her purse in a chair. "Let's get this over with."

Oh, this was starting beautifully. After he'd gotten the cold shoulder all through rehearsal, Myles suspected he'd made a serious miscalculation. Time to fix that. "Okay, before we go any further with this, I've had a little time to think about how I came off yesterday, and I want to assure you that I'm really not an asshole and have no intention of pressuring you for anything. This wasn't meant to force you into a corner or to break your personal rule about dating co-stars."

She narrowed her eyes. "Then what was it?"

"Teasing and curiosity. If you'd been cooler-headed, I wouldn't have known for sure I was right. But instead you dragged me into a closet." Where he'd had to exercise considerable restraint to keep his hands to himself because what else was he going to think about when trapped behind closed doors in an itty bitty space with a beautiful woman?

Piper studied him with speculation. "So you're saying you're letting me off the hook?"

Myles cringed. "At the risk of leaving my incorrigible curiosity unsatisfied...yes. I won't say anything to anybody. But you should know, the unsatisfied curiosity of a reporter is like the intellectual equivalent of blue balls. I'm hoping you'll have mercy on my brain."

She snorted as he'd hoped she would. It was such fun saying outrageous things to get a reaction out of her.

"It's such a fine brain, I hate to be that cruel. Especially about something that you could probably dig up yourself if you knew the right people to ask. The back story isn't too much of a secret around town."

"Then you'll stay for dinner? Tell me the story, while I cook for you?"

"I'll stay for dinner and tell you the story, while I help you cook. I can't just sit with idle hands."

"I can work with that." Myles led her back to the kitchen and began pulling ingredients out of the fridge and pantry.

"What are we having?"

"I figured a nice simple stir fry. Easy to customize based on personal preference and fast. What do you like?"

"Everything. But not too spicy."

"No Thai chilies then." He grabbed a bamboo cutting board and pulled a vegetable cleaver from the knife block. "Can I trust you with this?"

She arched those delicate brows and put on an innocent face. "I don't know, can you?"

"I'm watching you, Parish." He set an onion, bell pepper, zucchini, and some mushrooms beside her, and turned away to start rice in the cooker.

"So, you already know that there's history between Brody and Tyler."

"Charlotte told me they were the theater's golden couple, and then he up and broke her heart."

"That's the short, very uncomplicated version. I've known Brody forever. We started in theater around the same time. Tyler came later." The steady *crunch, thunk* of the knife punctuated her narrative. "Our senior year of high school, she won the role of Laurie in *Oklahoma*. Brody was Curly. They'd known each other for years. This is a small town, so that was unavoidable. But they'd never actually thought about each other like that until they hit the stage together. That show was...unparalleled. Because they really did fall in love as Laurie and Curly did and the audience could feel it. Their chemistry was undeniable. People still talk about that performance all these years later."

Myles set the oil to heat in a large wok and began slicing pork chops into bite-sized pieces. "I guess that wasn't one of those false intimacies."

"No. It was the real deal. They were inseparable after that. And so freaking perfect for each other, it was hard to remember they hadn't always been together. Seeing them dance together, hearing them sing... I'm good. Tucker's good. Tyler and Brody, when they played together, were professional quality. If they'd wanted, they could've taken Broadway by storm."

What he'd seen this last week hadn't come anywhere approaching professional quality.

As if sensing his thoughts, she looked up from the thin strips of bell pepper. "I can see that look of doubt on your face. You have to remember that this was before."

"What happened?"

Piper sighed. "Brody's parents were killed in a car accident our senior year of college. He fell apart. Went to a seriously dark place. Tyler took care of him, handled all the details, even though it gutted her, too. She'd lost her mom to breast cancer in high school, so she'd been really tight with Mrs. Jensen. We thought, maybe, things were getting better when she convinced him to go out for *Grease*. Of course they got the leads. That was the default back then. By the time the show was over, Brody seemed more like himself, like he was finally starting to heal. And then a week after the show closed, he just disappeared. No note, no phone call, no nothing. Tyler actually called out the police, sure something awful had happened to him. It was months before she had proof he wasn't dead in a ditch. And it wasn't because he'd contacted her himself but because he'd arranged for a management company to deal with leasing his parents' house."

"Ouch." He slid the meat into the waiting oil, listening to the sizzle and pop.

"She was devastated. And until this show, she hasn't set foot on stage since. It's been eight years, and she hasn't moved on."

"So when Brody showed back up...?"

"At first Tucker and I thought the best tactic would be keeping them separated. I'm the one who pushed her into auditioning. I'm the one who got her in this position in the first place." She passed him the bowl of chopped vegetables, separated out by how long each would take to cook.

Fishing out the pork and setting it aside, Myles began adding veggies to the wok. "What changed your mind?"

"He did. I can see how he looks at her. I don't know why he left or even, really, why he came back. But he still looks at her with his heart in his eyes. And Tyler wouldn't be so upset if she felt nothing. As long as Brody was the understudy, she could more or less avoid him. Avoidance wasn't going to fix anything. They need to work out their crap. Whatever the hell it is. So Tucker agreed to take one for the team so that Brody would have to take his place and Tyler would finally have to face him."

"The theatrical equivalent of locking them in a room together until they kill each other or learn to play nice." He added the meat back to the pan. "Here, stir this for a bit while I throw together sauce."

Piper took the wooden spoon. "Something like that."

"So what is it you hope to accomplish with this little ruse?" Soy sauce, brown sugar, some melted butter. Myles whisked the combination together before adding it to the pan.

Piper gave the lot of it a good stir before setting the spoon aside to let the sauce bubble and thicken. "I don't know. A happy ending would be nice. God knows she deserves it. But...resolution at the very least. Closure. Whichever way it goes, she never got that before, and she's never going to move on with her life until she gets it."

Myles considered the situation. "Your heart's in the right place, and I agree, the chemistry is apparently there, but there's too much bad history between them. They need to be reminded of the good."

"How?"

The first inklings of a plan began to percolate in the back of his brain as he pulled out plates, dishing up rice and dumping the fragrant stir fry over the top. "Well, you've already manipulated them this far. Are you up for a little more?"

"Possibly." She followed him over to the table and picked up chopsticks instead of the fork he'd set out, just in case. "What did you have in mind?"

They toasted with chopsticks. "We'll need to loop in Tucker."

Speakeasy was packed. Every table was full, and dozens of other patrons crowded around, waiting for the show. Whether Myles' plan worked on Tyler and Brody or not, Piper was forced to admit that the fund-raising aspect of it would definitely help out the Madrigal. The cast had commandeered the row of tables closest to the tiny stage. Brody sat camped out dead center, but there was no sign of Tyler.

Myles materialized out of the crowd. "Everything's set. The request list is pre-populated with duet requests for Tyler and Brody, and the donation jar has been seeded with some cash already to get things rolling."

"That's great. But what happens if Tyler doesn't show?" What the hell had Tucker been thinking, sending Brody to break the news about the fundraiser?

"Don't worry, she'll be here. Tucker's on it."

"What if we're wrong?"

"We're not," Myles assured her.

Piper caught her lip between her teeth. "But what if—"

He gripped her shoulders. "Hey. It's going to be okay."

Those hands slid down her arms and squeezed her hands. The

gesture comforted her, reminding her that she wasn't in this alone. Grateful, she turned her hands to clasp his and squeezed back. Someone moving past bumped into her, sending her stumbling into Myles.

His eyes met hers and his lips curved in that slow, melted caramel grin. It was the prop closet all over again. Heat and humor and that damnable pull.

You have the rule for a reason. But as she looked up at him, mouth not more than an inch from his, Piper was having a really hard time remembering what that reason was.

Before she could do something stupid, like lean in to kiss him right in the middle of the pizzeria in front of God and a goodly portion of the population of Wishful, a cheer rose up from the door, spreading through the crowd.

"And there's our girl," said Myles.

Piper took a deliberate step back, missing his touch the moment he released her hands. "It's show time."

Tyler looked dazed as she trailed Tucker and his crutches through the crowd, blindly accepting handshakes and well wishes. She'd clearly forgotten how beloved she'd been. Tonight would be a good reminder, Piper decided.

"Hey there, everybody! Who's ready for some music?" Tucker, official emcee for the night, grinned at the crowd.

More cheers and claps. Piper and Myles joined the rest of the cast and a handful of other folks she'd acted with in the past as Tucker launched into his spiel, waving a hand at the marker board mounted on an easel beside the stage.

"So here's how this is gonna work. We've got our performers listed in tiers. The more you love 'em, the more it'll cost to have them sing for you. The bottom tier will cost you five bucks per song per person. The top is pricier. Twenty bucks per song, per person. You want a duet, you get to pick who sings it and pay for the pair. Group stuff, same deal. We encourage you to pool your funds and remember that this is for a good cause, so don't be shy!

You can pick anything in the book over here. We'll start off with a freebie to kick off the night. This one's for everybody."

On cue, Piper and the others crowded onto the stage. People were already lining up, cash and checkbooks in hand. At least half a dozen people stuffed money in Tucker's jar as they kicked things off with a rousing rendition of "Any Way You Want It."

Piper was first on deck after the group dispersed to the clutch of tables up front. As she launched into "Diamonds Are a Girl's Best Friend", she was gratified to see Brody drop into a chair next to Tyler. They had actual conversation without trying to kill each other. Progress.

In response to whistles and applause, Piper took her bow and handed off the mic to Tyler for her first solo of the night, "Maybe This Time" from *Cabaret*. Off to the side, Rick Stevens figured out how to operate the lights on the tiny stage and spotlit her for it.

Piper shot him a thumbs up and fell into Tyler's vacated chair. "I didn't think she'd come."

"You know she's not going to let the Madrigal down," Brody said, not taking his eyes off her. "It's too big a part of her history."

It was too big a part of her history with *him*, which was why she'd worried. But Piper wasn't going to open that can of worms with Brody.

Even without the pre-seeded list, the crowd kept Tyler and Brody steadily busy. Tyler started off a bit stiff during "We Go Together" from *Grease*. But she made Ethel Merman proud as she dueled with Brody on "Anything You Can Do." By the time they rotated into Garth Brooks/Trisha Yearwood duets, she'd hit her stride, having fun and playing the crowd, sparking off Brody in a way she hadn't done in years.

Piper guzzled a glass of lemon water and leaned toward Myles. "I think it's working!"

"C'mon. We're up." He tugged her to her feet.

"We are? Singing what?"

"'Quando, Quando, Quando'. Bublé and Nelly Furtado."

"Who signed us up for that?" she asked.

Myles grinned back at her and offered a mic. "Who do you think?"

She couldn't help but laugh. "So it's like that, is it?"

His only answer was to take her hand and jerk her into him with a spin. As he began to croon, he began to move. Following the subtle pressure on her hip, Piper fell into his rhythm, grinning as she recognized a slow cha cha. He wasn't smooth like Tucker or electric like Brody, but for an improv number, Myles was pretty damned good. She sang her response, getting into the dance with some undulating hip action that had the crowd whistling. He upped the ante again, taking a firmer grip on her hip and following the motion of her body, and Piper forgot about the crowd, able to focus only on the man and the music.

As they sang the final notes, Myles brought Piper to a stop. Her eyes were dilated, the pulse in her throat hammering, and it took everything he had not to take her mouth right then and there. Applause broke the spell.

She recovered first, turning toward the crowd with a laugh. "Myles Stewart, ladies and gentlemen! Our Bob Wallace is a man of hidden talents."

Understanding his cue, Myles gave a sweeping bow.

They vacated the stage for Tucker. Myles wanted to pull Piper into the hallway, outside, anywhere but in the middle of all these freaking people. But she went back to her seat. Resigned, he followed.

After doing Nat King Cole proud with his rendition of "L-O-V-E", Tucker made way for Tyler. As the opening notes of "It's All Coming Back To Me Now" began to play, she looked out at the audience and arched a brow. "Really?" Somebody cheered from back near the door. Tyler just shook her head and offered up a little wave as she launched into the song, hamming it up, and wringing every ounce of parodied emotion out of the piece.

Brody didn't seem to be amused by the performance. The poor guy looked like he'd been gut punched, white-faced and a little sick. What was that about?

When Tyler finished, Brody met her at the edge of the stage to take the mic. He murmured something that had her frowning before she returned to her table. The music started and something in the room palpably shifted as Brody fixed his gaze on Tyler and began to sing, "I'll Stand By You."

This. This is what Piper was talking about.

Myles watched, as captivated as everyone else in the room, while Brody serenaded Tyler with a sincerity that evoked all the feels, as his sister would say. Through it all, Tyler sat, cheeks flushed, twitching in her seat.

When he finished, the crowd went nuts, rising to a full-on standing ovation. Eyes still on her, Brody stepped off the stage, passing the mic off to Myles. Tyler was up in a second, jerking her head toward the fire exit and the alley. Without a word, Brody followed.

"Oh boy," muttered Piper.

"That's either really good or really bad," Myles observed.

"I can't stand it." She broke away from the crowd of singers and cut toward the front door.

Myles tossed the mic to Charlotte and trailed after her. "Piper, you're going to freeze in that dress."

"Don't care."

"You can't just eavesdrop on them."

"This from a newspaperman?" She spared him a bare glance of disbelief. "What kind of reporter are you?"

She had him there. Giving up, he followed her outside, sneaking around to the alley that ran behind Speakeasy. They peered through the space between one of the employees' cars and the wall as Tyler's laugher rang out.

Hands clasping hers, Brody's face was serious. "I hardly think this is a laughing matter."

That just elicited another round of giggling.

Oh Jesus, he didn't do something stupid like propose, did he?

Tyler managed to choke down her mirth long enough to get out, "Brody, Ollie is my dog."

"Your...dog," Brody said. "But I heard you talking, at the shop earlier, saw the toys, and I thought..." He trailed off.

The smile was still in her voice as she said, "You thought he was my son. That he was *our* son."

"I...yeah." There was no mistaking the disappointment on his face.

Tyler's laughter died. "Brody, honey, did you honestly think it was possible that I could've had a child, *your* child, and somehow you wouldn't have known about it? That I would have kept such a thing from you, if it were true?"

He released her to scrub both hands over his face. "Okay, yeah, when you put it that way, it does sound ridiculous. But I just... from what you said it sounded like you were talking to a child. And then he was seven. And..."

"You leapt to some really impressive conclusions. Why didn't you just ask outright? If not me, then Tucker or Piper. They could've told you otherwise."

"I figured if they hadn't told me, it was for a reason. Same with you. I... I'm sorry for making things weird. God, you must think I'm an idiot."

In the face of his supreme embarrassment, something in Tyler's expression softened. "Doesn't have to be weird if we don't let it be. Come on, I'm sure there's a list another mile long of requests waiting for us." She held out a hand, probably the first gesture of peace and welcome she'd made to him since he got back. When he took it, she pulled him in for a hug. "Thank you."

"For what?"

"For wanting to do the right thing."

As soon as the door slapped shut behind them, Piper surged up from her crouch, flinging her arms around Myles' neck and hugging him tight. "Your plan worked!" She kissed him, a quick smacking thing, ended on a bubbling laugh almost before it was begun.

Myles was out of self-restraint. As he slid his arms around her, Piper's delight shifted to confusion, then awareness. He didn't give her time to pull away before capturing that mouth he'd been dreaming about for weeks. If she'd pushed him away, he'd have let her go. Reluctantly, but he'd have managed. Instead she slid her fingers into his hair and opened for him on a sigh.

That almost instant acquiescence fired his blood, had him wanting all of her in fast, greedy bites before starting all over again. But he'd been waiting too damned long for this, so he forced himself to slow down, keep the tone slow and easy, with just a hint of an edge to remind her that he wasn't the mild-mannered music producer he played on stage.

He'd wanted this, wanted to taste her mouth in private, before they crossed that line in whatever fashion Nate deemed appropriate for the show. She tasted of the lemon water she'd been drinking all night. There was nothing of the timid Betty Haynes about her now. She was the one who dove deeper, pulling him under with a sexy little moan that had his control fraying.

Myles had just enough sanity left to remember where they were. In an alley, only a few dozen feet away from their entire cast of co-stars and a good portion of the entire town. With his last shreds of control, he eased back. Piper stared up at him, cheeks flushed, lips wet and red. Her breath wasn't altogether steady. As he watched, awareness seeped back in for her, too. Before she could say anything—like *This was a mistake*—Myles spoke. "Tyler and Brody aren't the only ones who make a good team on stage and off."

For the first time since he'd met her, Piper Parish was speechless. And it was pretty damned adorable.

He chucked her under the chin and stepped back before he dove back in where they'd left off. "I've got a late night to put the paper to bed properly, but I'll see you at rehearsal, Betty. Meanwhile, I'll be dreaming of March 20th. And so will you."

Whistling, Myles walked away, leaving his lovely leading lady staring after him.

JUST FOR THIS MOMENT

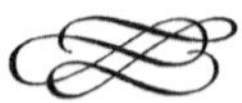

WISHFUL ROMANCE # 4

A madcap modern marriage of convenience tale sure to leave fans begging for more

Maybe there hasn't been actual blood, other than a few paper cuts, but Myles has put plenty of sweat into his independent, local newspaper, and he's even willing to admit to a few manly tears. Certainly, the paper has been his mistress since he moved to the small town of Wishful, Mississippi, and he doesn't feel it's hyperbolic in the least to say it owns a piece of his soul. He's building his dream, independent of the life laid out for him by his family, and that means everything. There's nothing he wouldn't do to ensure its success.

Piper fell hard for Myles when they co-stared in the production of *White Christmas* that saved Wishful's historic Madrigal Theater. Not in love, she's careful to remind herself, but into very serious like, and certainly outrageous, chemistry-fueled attraction. But Piper knows that the bright lights of the stage can wreak havoc with perspective. She's been burnt by them before, when an on-stage passion fizzled into disappointment and heartache. That's why she put on the brakes with Myles, and she admits to herself that the fact that he played by her rules and waited only adds to his appeal.

When Myles tells her that a major investor is pulling out of the paper, leaving him with a huge loan to repay or lose his control over what he's built, Piper is devastated for him. But when he jokingly admits that the best option he's come up with is to marry a showgirl to gain access to a trust fund, well, that just sounds like a plan to Piper. After all, why not take this great guy on marriage test drive? He's worth having just for this moment, however long it lasts. But as their fake marriage turns alarmingly real, they'll have to decide if they're in it for the moment or forever.

Chapter One

"*W*ELL? WHAT DO YOU think?" Myles Stewart sat across the table, trying to read the inscrutable face of his lunch companion.

Simone chased the bite of muffaletta with sweet tea and lifted her arm to get the attention of their waitress.

Corinne wandered over, more sass in the sway of her hips than she'd had when Myles moved to Wishful seven months before. He hadn't gotten the story on her yet. "Get you a refill on that tea, hon?"

"I'd like to speak to the cook."

"Something wrong with your sandwich?" Corinne asked.

"I'd just like to speak to the cook," Simone said evenly.

With a worried frown, the waitress headed back to the kitchen.

"What are you doing, Simone?"

She just lifted a sardonic brow and continued to sip her tea.

Myles glanced back to the kitchen where Mama Pearl Buckley, Goddess of Pie and Gossip and owner of Dinner Belles Diner, stepped through the door. Her brows drew down in thundercloud formation as she looked Simone's way.

Oh, this is not good. Not good at all.

"Seriously, if something's wrong, they'll fix it. There's no need to call Omar out."

"Omar, huh?"

Omar Buckley, master of the kitchen and Mama Pearl's youngest son, pushed into the room, a grease spattered apron stretched across abs that were just as flat as they'd been when he'd played on scholarship as running back for Ole Miss eight years ago—before the knee injury that blew his football career. Myles had heard that sad tale over coffee several months back. Omar's face was a twin of his mother's, and he had the shoulders and arms to back up his displeasure.

Shit. The last thing Myles needed was Simone making enemies her first day on the job. Myles could see the headline now. *Out-of-Towner Earns Buckley Wrath—Banned From Diner for Life.*

The lunch crowd went silent as Omar's shadow fell over the table. Everyone waited with baited breath to see how things would unfold.

"Somethin' I can do for you? Ma'am." This last he added after a pause.

Simone tipped her head back, blatantly scanning him from head to toe and back again, her lovely, mocha-colored face absolutely deadpan. "Omar, I presume?"

"Yeah."

"I just wanted to shake the hand of the man who made the best damned muffaletta I've had outside the French Quarter."

Myles released an audible breath.

The tension in Omar's face smoothed into a grin. "That a fact?"

"I lived there for close to ten years, so I'm in a position to know." She offered her hand. "Simone Grayson."

Omar took it, his bigger palm swallowing Simone's. "You visiting?"

"New in town. Glad to know I'll be able to satisfy at least some of my culinary cravings for N'Awlins."

Now that the threat was past, Omar made his own lazy survey of Simone, ending with an expression that said he'd be happy to satisfy any craving she had, culinary or otherwise. And Simone wasn't shutting him down. Wasn't that interesting?

As the silence stretched out between them, charging like a freaking Duracell, Myles fell back on old social training for proper introductions. "Simone's the new full-time reporter for *The Observer*."

"That right?"

"Omar does a bi-monthly food column for the paper. He rotates out with Tom Thatcher from The Spring House."

"I look forward to testing out some of your recipes."

"You do that. And if you have a hankering for somethin' in particular, you let me know. I might can do somethin' about it."

Simone smiled, and Myles was put in mind of a cat that'd cornered a particularly tasty form of prey. "I'll keep that in mind. Thanks."

As Omar headed back to the kitchen, Simone dove into her muffaletta in earnest.

"You need a cold shower?" Myles asked. "Because I'm pretty sure you just cranked up the temperature in here a good fifteen degrees."

She shrugged. "Let's just say I'm more than a little glad I let you talk me away from *The Times-Picayune*."

"And I consider that one of my greatest coups. I told you you'd love it here."

His phone dinged, signaling a reminder. Myles slid it from his pocket and glanced at the screen. **Call Piper up for a date**.

Myles couldn't stop the grin from stretching ear to ear.

Finally.

He'd met Piper last September, during auditions for the Wishful Community Theater production of *White Christmas*. As

Bob to her Betty, he'd held her, kissed her, spent hours with her on set and off. And he'd gone more than half crazy for her in the process. But the lovely and talented Piper Parish did not date her co-stars. Some B.S. about the false intimacy of the stage, which had seemed reasonable at the time he'd agreed to it. He'd been waiting three months. Months where they didn't get to hang out or talk more than the occasional text. Well, and the monthly karaoke night up at Speakeasy Pizzeria. The woman *loved* her karaoke and damned if he hadn't gone and learned half the music from Broadway just for the chance to sing with her. But that was more a group thing, not a one-on-one hang out opportunity. So he'd kept waiting. Ninety long, lonely days for her self-imposed edict to pass. And now, time was up.

Hot damn.

Maybe he could swing by the clinic where she worked to ask her in person before he headed back to the paper.

"You're looking awfully happy."

"Why wouldn't I be happy? I stole one of the most talented reporters I've ever had the pleasure of working with from one of the best papers in the country, I'm having a damned fine cheeseburger for lunch, and the paper is finally turning an actual profit."

"A good thing, too, as I'd like to actually get paid."

No sooner had Myles shoved the phone back into his pocket, then it beeped again, this time with an incoming text. He fished it out and read the message from his general Jill-of-All-Trades, Patty Hamilton, who he'd inherited when he bought *The Wishful Observer*.

Patty: **Your investor's attorney is here.**

Myles frowned.

"Something wrong?" Simone asked.

"Not sure." He texted Patty back. **Did we have a meeting scheduled?**

Patty: **No. He won't say what it's about.**

He? Not the usual woman?

Patty: **No. Never seen this one. According to his card, he's one of the partners from her firm in Atlanta.**

That was...odd and more than a little disconcerting. What could he want?

Be there as soon as I finish up lunch.

Looked like he wouldn't get the chance to swing by the clinic to see Piper after all.

Because he didn't want to wait, he thumbed a quick text to Piper. **Time's up, Buttercup. When can I see you?**

Like some love-struck teenager, he stared at the phone, hoping to see the little gray bubble with dancing ellipses that would indicate an immediate reply. But there was nothing. And hell, the clinic could be under a rush with God knew what. They were smack dab in the middle of prime-time sinus infection season. She wasn't about to be texting when she was supposed to be taking blood pressure or temperatures or giving somebody a shot.

Calling himself an idiot, he put the phone away and finished inhaling his lunch. Simone got the rest of hers to go—which came complete with Omar's number scrawled on the Styrofoam box—and they hot-footed it across the town green and down the street to the humble offices of *The Wishful Observer*.

Myles didn't let himself get uptight or worried. His investor probably just wanted another progress report or additional explanation of some of the expansions Myles wanted to make. The hotshot lawyer out of Atlanta was probably just stopping by because he was on his way to somewhere else.

Right, because Wishful is so on the beaten path?

By the time he stepped through the doors, Myles was willing to concede he felt a little bit nervous about the drop-in meeting. Those infantile nerves turned into awkward tweenagers at the sight of Patty's face.

"What?" he asked her.

"He's in the conference room. Just sitting there like an extra in a *Terminator* movie."

"Are we talking T-800 here or T-1000?"

"Tough call. I wasn't brave enough to try to kosh him over the head to see if he liquefied to fix himself."

Simone looked impressed. "You know *Terminator*?"

"Please. I have three sons. I don't know what he wants, Myles, but be careful in there."

Wanting to reassure her, he squeezed Patty's shoulder. "It'll be fine."

Stepping into the small conference room, Myles thought perhaps this guy should've auditioned as an extra for *The Matrix*. He looked like a better dressed Agent Smith, and Myles half expected to see an earwig partially covered by the perfectly cut brown hair.

"Mr. Stewart." When the words didn't come out with the same measured tone as Mr. Anderson, Myles was almost disappointed. This guy had a cultured, country club Southern drawl—the kind of accent Myles could imagine him practicing in front of a bathroom mirror, while quoting Atticus Finch.

"That would be me. I'm afraid you have me at a disadvantage, sir."

"I'm John Bondurant, from Bondurant, Meadows, and Leach. I'm here on behalf of your investor."

He didn't offer his hand to shake, so Myles dropped into a chair. "Of course. What can I do for you, Mr. Bondurant?"

"My client has reviewed the latest progress reports you forwarded on and is, quite frankly, disappointed in the profit and loss statements."

As unease slithered through him, Myles wished desperately they were in his office, where his desk was covered in toys he could pick up to occupy his hands. What he would give for a Slinky just now. "I realize the profit margin is a bit thin right now, but I've had less than a year to get the paper turned around. Some of the equipment needed updating, and I've had to expand my staff to accommodate the increased workload." If you could call moving from three employees to four and adding a high school intern a real staff expansion.

"Nevertheless, my client is concerned that your rather…ambitious plans are more optimistic than realistic."

"Change takes time. And businesses of any variety require solid investment before they really have an opportunity to grow." How many times had he heard that refrain growing up? Damn it, he knew business, and he knew newspapers. What he was doing here was working. Rome wasn't built in a friggin' day.

Mr. Bondurant pulled a folder from his shiny leather briefcase. "My function today is as messenger, Mr. Stewart. You needn't justify yourself to me."

Eying the folder like it would bite him, Myles slowly reached out and took it. There were only a few sheets inside. He pulled his reading glasses from his inside jacket pocket and read through the papers, feeling his cheeseburger congeal and harden with every word.

"This is insane. I can't possibly have the full payment on the loan by then. That's not even two months! This isn't what we agreed to."

"On the contrary, my client is exercising the right to pull out of the investment. In light of last quarter's returns, my client is well within rights according to the original agreement."

"Well, we need to revisit the damned agreement, then. This is ludicrous. I want to talk to your client. Directly."

"That's not possible. My client deals only with proxies. I'd be happy to take your counter offer back and present it, but I advise you, Mr. Stewart, to begin looking for other investors. The loan payment is due at the end of the forty-five days or you forfeit ownership of the paper."

～

"THEY'LL MAKE such beautiful babies, with her pretty face. Better hope for a boy first because those girls will be so pretty, they'll need a big brother to beat the boys off."

Why did I let Mom and Leah talk me into this?

Piper Parish sat in the middle of a long table at the Wishful Country Club, as black-and-white clad wait staff wove around the bridal party, removing the salad plates—spinach and strawberry salad with poppyseed dressing, of course—contemplating whether it might be more enjoyable to stab herself in the eye with her salad fork, as she listened to her Great Aunt Beatrice extol the virtues of the bride-to-be. Carrie Jo was a jobless, twenty-two-year-old, barely out of college, who had no actual aspiration in life beyond getting her MRS degree, which she'd be achieving on Saturday. She was also Piper's cousin, which was exactly how Piper had been roped into being part of the bridal party. Considering she had actually changed Carrie Jo's diapers, that was a little bit demoralizing.

As the main course appeared—nothing but chicken salad would do for a bridesmaids' luncheon—Piper wondered if she could get away with ordering a mimosa or three in the name of celebration. Given this was the Southern Baptist side of the family, she thought not.

More's the pity.

"I heard Richard wants her to stay home so they can go ahead and start trying for a family."

Yeah, that's because they already got started on that part.

Not that Carrie Jo had mentioned it. But as a nurse, Piper was well-attuned to the signs. That glow sure as hell wasn't wedding happies. She wasn't showing yet, and Piper was reasonably sure no one else in the family knew or suspected. Considering the holy hell that would break loose if they found out—at least before Saturday—Piper wasn't about to be the one to reveal that secret. Let Carrie Jo have her day with as little drama as possible.

"So, when are we going to be hearing wedding bells for you,

Piper?" Aunt Bea asked. "You've already let Leah beat you on that one."

Piper sipped at her sweet tea and muttered. "Last time I checked, marriage wasn't NASCAR." Not that anybody in her family recognized that fact. Her baby sister had beat her in the race to the altar three years prior, at the ripe young age of twenty-four. And she'd delighted the entire family by immediately providing the first grandchild a year later. A boy, Preston, who, Piper was forced to admit, was cute as the dickens. Leah was winning points left and right.

The remark earned her an aggravated look from her mother. It was an expression Piper was intimately familiar with.

"What's that, dear?" her great aunt asked.

"Nothing. No wedding bells for me any time soon, Aunt Bea."

"Oh, that's a shame. But surely there's someone special?"

Because the idea that her life could revolve around something other a man certainly didn't compute.

Before Piper could think of a snark-free reply to that, her phone vibrated. It was purely verboten that she had it out of her purse at all, but if she was caught, she had the excuse of being on-call at the clinic. Not that she actually was today, but they didn't know that.

She slid the phone from beneath her napkin and swiped to unlock the screen.

Myles: **Time's up, Buttercup. When can I see you?**

Piper's cheeks warmed, and she had to fight back the grin tugging at her lips.

Speaking of someone special.

The new-in-town and very sexy Myles Stewart had been her unexpected co-star in last fall's production of *White Christmas*. He'd been at auditions to write a story about the show and decided to audition himself just for the chance to meet her. She'd spent the last months of autumn fighting the zing between them, sticking to her self-imposed rule about not dating her romantic lead. He hadn't blinked when she'd issued a cool-down period so that whatever intimacy engendered by the show could fade. Instead, he'd spent the entire three months sending her outrageous texts and a daily notice of the countdown. She'd done her best not to respond too often, encourage him too much. But those texts had been the highlight of her days, keeping that zing alive and well and impatient. And then there was karaoke night. She lived for the chance to sing with him. They'd been carrying on the subtle flirtation through song all these months.

And now the wait was over.

Thank God.

Her thumb hovered over the screen, prepared to tap out a reply—*Is now too soon?*

"Piper!" The sound of her mother's voice almost made Piper drop the phone. "Are you on your phone?"

"No ma'am. I was just checking in with the clinic." Reluctantly, she slid the phone back into her purse beneath her mother's disapproving eye. She'd be hearing about this later.

Just as well she hadn't answered yet. Between work and all the wedding events, she wouldn't actually be free until after Saturday. Maybe Saturday night if the reception didn't run too late.

"What were you saying about who you were dating?" Aunt Bea asked.

Of course she hadn't lost that line of questioning.

Piper considered saying something about Myles, but the last thing she wanted was any of her nosy relatives going to bother him at work to find out who his people were. Besides, they weren't dating. Yet.

"I haven't had a lot of time for dating lately. We just recently wrapped the production of *The Mousetrap*." She didn't usually go out for the non-musical roles, but she'd needed the distraction to keep from giving in to the temptation to blow her rule all to hell and jump straight into things with Myles—which, given the level of that zing, would likely have led straight to bed, thus breaking another personal rule. "Were you able to make it out to see the show? We got rave reviews."

"That's nice, honey, but you really should devote more time to finding yourself a husband. That biological clock is ticking and you don't have all that much time left."

"Right, because my ability to pop out babies is my only valuable attribute as a woman, and, at twenty-nine, I'm ancient and my uterus is populated by dust and cobwebs."

"Piper Elizabeth!" Her mother's middle name invocation brought all conversations at the table to a screeching halt. Nearly a dozen pairs of eyes fixed on her.

At Twyla's look of censure, Piper ducked her head. "Sorry, Mama."

This was her longest standing and most challenging role to date. Pretending to give a damn about what the rest of her family thought she ought to be doing with her life. Because certainly what she actually wanted didn't matter to any of them. God forbid she be anything but the traditional, dutiful, meek Southern daughter.

Carrie Jo's mama jumped into the conversational breach. "Piper, I'm just going over some last-minute details with the caterer," Jolene waved her own cell phone and nobody got on to her. "I think your reply card got lost in the mail. Do you have a plus one for the reception?"

This just keeps getting better and better.

She nearly said yes. For two long seconds, Piper considered asking Myles if he'd be her plus one. She doubted he'd say no and, God knew, his company would make the wedding less of a misery for her. But then her family would know about him. And he'd know about her family. Neither of those things seemed likely to lead to a desire for him to spend more time with her. Better to suck it up and admit the truth.

"No ma'am, I don't."

"Oh, that's a shame."

Piper called on all her acting chops to keep her smile fixed in place and set in polite rather than feral lines.

Carrie Joe's Aunt Rae spoke up. "I could set you up with Forest Langford. He's getting out again since his divorce."

"What about Quincy Blackmon?" Libby Newsom, the maid of honor, suggested.

Piper lifted a hand to stop the commentary and offers of pity dates. "No, really, it's all right. I avoided having a plus one on purpose."

They all stared at her as if she'd sprouted a second head.

"I just thought I could be of more help if I wasn't having to entertain a date. There's so much to manage, after all." A blatant lie, but it effectively turned the tide of pity.

"Well, isn't that just the sweetest thing?" Jolene declared. "Since you're…unencumbered, can I get you to—"

As Jolene took advantage of Piper's slip up to pile on additional wedding duties, all Piper could do was grin and bear it.

Three more days. Three more days and this insanity is over.

Grab your copy of *Just For This Moment* today!

- *Made For Loving You* (Paisley and Ty)

MEN OF THE MISFIT INN
SMALL TOWN SOUTHERN ROMANCE

- *Let It Be Me* (Emerson and Caleb)
- *Our Kind of Love* (Abbey and Kyle)

WISHFUL SERIES
SMALL TOWN SOUTHERN ROMANCE

- *Once Upon A Coffee* (Avery and Dillon)
- *To Get Me To You* (Cam and Norah)
- *Know Me Well* (Liam and Riley)
- *Be Careful, It's My Heart* (Brody and Tyler)
- *Just For This Moment* (Myles and Piper)
- *Wish I Might* (Reed and Cecily)
- *Turn My World Around* (Tucker and Corinne)
- *Dance Me A Dream* (Jace and Tara)
- *See You Again* (Trey and Sandy)
- *The Christmas Fountain* (Chad and Mary Alice)
- *You Were Meant For Me* (Mitch and Tess)
- *A Lot Like Christmas* (Ryan and Hannah)
- *Dancing Away With My Heart* (Zach and Lexi)

WISHING FOR A HERO SERIES (A WISHFUL SPINOFF SERIES)
SMALL TOWN ROMANTIC SUSPENSE

- *Make You Feel My Love* (Judd and Autumn)
- *Watch Over Me* (Nash and Rowan)
- *Can't Take My Eyes Off You* (Ethan and Miranda)
- *Burn For You* (Sean and Delaney)

MEET CUTE ROMANCE

SMALL TOWN SHORT ROMANCE

- *Once Upon A Snow Day*
- *Once Upon A New Year's Eve*
- *Once Upon An Heirloom*
- *Once Upon A Coffee*
- *Once Upon A Campfire*
- *Once Upon A Rescue*

SUMMER CAMP
CONTEMPORARY ROMANCE

- *Once Upon A Campfire*
- *Second Chance Summer*

ACKNOWLEDGMENTS

THIS BOOK WOULD not have been possible without the unwavering support of my critique partners, Susan Bischoff and Claire Legrand. They gave me encouragement and butt kicking as necessary to get me from my "Once upon a time..." to "The end" and were completely supportive of my jumping ship from my paranormal roots to try something new.

Thanks to my cover artist, Robin Ludwig, who regularly amazes me by taking images straight out of my brain and putting them together for the rest of the world to enjoy.

I would also like to offer up special thanks to the baristas at 929 Coffee, who provided smiles, fabulous biscuits, and endless cups of tea to fuel my creative drive. Y'all are the best!

Kait is a Mississippi native, who often swears like a sailor, calls everyone sugar, honey, or darlin', and can wield a bless your heart like a saber or a Snuggie, depending on requirements.

You can find more information on this RITA ® Award-winning author and her books on her website http:// kaitnolan.com. While you're there, sign up for her newsletter so you don't miss out on news about new releases!

9 781648 350030